Outlaw Bodies

A speculative fiction anthology
edited by

Lori Selke
&
Djibril al-Ayad

Outlaw Bodies
First published 2012 by Futurefire.net Publishing
All stories © 2012 the authors
Cover illustration © 2012 Robin E. Kaplan

Vylar Kaftan's "She Called Me Baby" was first published in *Strange Horizons* 30 May 2005, and is © Vylar Kaftan, 2005.
M. Svairini's "Mouth" was first published in *Up For Grabs 2: None of the Above,* ed. Lauren P. Burka, Circlet Press, 2011, and is © M. Svairini, 2011.
Emily Capettini's "Elmer Bank", Anna Caro's "Millie", Fabio Fernandes's "The Remaker", Lori Selke's "Frankenstein Unraveled" and introduction, Stacy Sinclair's "Winds: NW 20 km/hr", Jo Thomas's "Good Form", Tracie Welser's "Her Bones, Those of the Dead" and Kathryn Allan's afterword are all published here for the first time, and are © the authors, 2012.

ISBN-print: 978-0-9573975-0-7
ISBN-electronic: 978-0-9573975-1-4

Contact:
editor@futurefire.net
http://futurefire.net/

Contents

Introduction

Lori Selke

What is an outlaw body?

In a nutshell, any body that defies social norms and expectations. An outlaw body is not necessarily the same thing as an illegal body, although illegal bodies are certainly outlaw. How can a body be an illegal body? When bodies can be considered property of an individual or of the state, any body that defies those claims is an illegal body. More concretely: escaped slaves and draft dodgers are two forms of illegal bodies—as are illegitimate children. If the state regulates how you can modify your body, then illegally modified bodies are outlawed bodies. At one time, in certain cultures, bodies with tattoos were outlaw bodies. Anyone who has to hide their septum piercing from their day job is living with an outlaw body.

Outlaw bodies can also simply defy social and cultural expectations or move into spaces that the law does not accommodate. Genderqueer, gender-nonconforming and transgender/transsexual people live in outlaw bodies. Individuals with physical disabilities may experience their bodies as outlaw as well. Plastic surgery performance artists join athletes who have changed their physique using performance-enhancing drugs. If a body must belong to a state, then stateless people become outlaw bodies as well.

Sometimes, simply being brown or black is enough to make you an outlaw body, or at the very least a suspicious one. Stop and frisk. Show your papers. In a social justice context, talking of illegal bodies inevitably conjures up "stop using the I word" campaigns that aim to eliminate the slur "illegals" from mainstream media reporting about undocumented immigrants. "No human being is illegal" is one popular slogan of this movement.

Reproduction and fertility control is another site of social struggle, a place where bodies may be proclaimed outlaw by legal or social fiat. Prison, too, becomes a site where bodies are both regulated and resist regulation.

Now picture someone who commits a crime to gain access to needed or desired medical treatment. This could be as innocuous and gray-area as buying drugs from another country, as white-collar as insurance fraud, or as risky and dramatic as robbing a bank to pay the doctor's bills.

All of these examples are drawn from history or the present day. What about the future? What about hybrids, mutants, neural rewiring?

Machines that aspire to be human, and humans that aspire to be machine? In the future, we may see modifications made to conform to hostile environments—under the sea, elsewhere in the solar system, or in the spaces between stars. Will all of those changes be socially permitted, or will some be proscribed? Why? And what of those who pursue those changes regardless?

In this anthology, you will find artists, mothers, and academics; bodies constructed of flesh and of bone, of paper and metal and plastic. Bodies formed of bouncing, buzzing electrons, waves and particles of light. Bodies grown and bodies sewn, glued, folded and sutured. And all of them standing in defiance of the rules and regulations designed to bind them.

Like all the best fiction, imagining the outlaw bodies that the future might hold helps shine a light on the outlaw bodies we all live in today. Such stories expand the boundaries of what we might consider human. And the wider that space, the more breathing room for everyone. These stories show us new strategies of resistance—and provide new reasons as to why resistance is necessary. Vital. Essential.

Enjoy.

Lori Selke, co-editor

Good Form

Jo Thomas

DAY 1

"You're new," the man behind the desk said.

She nodded for politeness' sake, to show she'd heard.

"Name?"

"Astrid Lee."

The man called up records on his console. "Got you. Follow the blue lights to your assigned workshop. There'll be a control point along the way where you'll be asked to change into company overalls."

"Shouldn't there be some kind of induction?" Astrid asked, surprised.

The man smiled. "All you need to know was covered in the interview process and the paperwork you signed."

The blue light led her to the promised changing room then to a large room divided into six large workshops. Two were closed off, their glass dividers opaque and sound damped for privacy. Two were divided off but the glass remained clear. Two were open with boxed supplies on the desks and floor, and only one of those were occupied. The blue light led to the other.

"One week on days, one week twenty four hours a day, one week off," Astrid reminded herself.

The phrases "small team", "lone working" and "unique, quality product" had been bandied about when she had asked about the working conditions. Astrid hadn't cared. There was too much irony in being replaced with machines and then being employed to put other machines together.

"Hello," she said to her new cubicle neighbour, "I'm Astrid."

The pale, moon-faced woman looked over her shoulder. "Dianna. Unpack the limbs and lay them out on your bench so you can run basic diagnostics."

She turned back to her own boxes, leaving Astrid to do as she was told.

The first box was a muscular right arm. Astrid couldn't bring herself to take it from the plastic beads that protected it and, instead, opened the boxes holding the other arm and two equally well muscled legs. That done, she stared at the rich brown synthetic skin.

"Not seen a form before?" Dianna asked, watching.

Astrid forced a smile. "Yes, but only through windows."

Dianna turned back to her own work, to limbs that looked delicate and slender.

☣

DAY 2

"Torso today," Dianna said, and then turned back to her work.

Astrid opened the most likely of the two remaining boxes. She stared—the factory had gone as far as to ensure the chest had nipples—then pulled it out. She could feel the shape of ribs beneath her hands, under a fine layer of skin and muscle.

"All fake," she whispered.

She wanted to take her hand away and scrub it until she felt clean again, just as she had the night before.

"Oh, that one's hot!" Dianna said.

Astrid stopped, holding the torso away from herself at an awkward angle, and looked at her neighbour. Dianna held her form's hour-glass torso against herself, hands tight on two rounded buttocks.

"I'll swap," said Astrid.

"Why? You prefer women?"

"I just thought you'd find this one more interesting," Astrid said evenly, "You said he was hot."

She wished Dianna didn't enjoy the forms quite so much. Although she used to see more blatant behaviour from her former students, this was somehow much worse.

"We're matched up with the forms we're given," Dianna said. "No swaps or we ruin the final product."

They'd said as much when Astrid had been put through the battery of personality tests. Now she was starting to wonder if it had been worth it, if she should have ignored the suggestion from the employment agency, but she needed the job.

She turned away from Dianna and put the torso on the bench beside the limbs. She avoided looking at it as much as she could as she made the connections required to run diagnostics. Only when she had the programs running did she give in to curiosity and look down. She was relieved to see it was like any shop mannequin—sexless with nothing more than a bulge so clothes and accessories hung properly.

☣

DAY 3

"Head!" Dianna sang.

She stroked the torso, upright on her bench, with a little too much delight for Astrid's comfort. Telling herself that it was simply a cleverer version of a shop dummy only made her feel worse. They couldn't chose for themselves.

Dianna said, "We'll sort out hair when the diagnostics have run."

The form she was building clicked as the head was fitted to the torso. The head turned all the way round, both ways, and then went through various tilted positions.

Astrid copied her neighbour. It was harder than it had looked to make the connection and she almost screamed when it clicked because the eyes opened. She hadn't noticed Dianna's form do that and she hadn't realised the forms were given eyes that looked like metal balls. The ones in shop windows wore sunglasses.

Dianna laughed. "Just run the diagnostics."

Astrid turned to vent but saw Dianna stroking the other torso again, her fingers close to small, almost child-like breasts. Part of Astrid's brain wondered what the factory put under the synthetic skin to make breasts feel like breasts, if they felt like breasts. The rest just felt sickened.

"Please don't do that," she said.

Dianna looked at her with raised eyebrows. "Why not?"

Astrid couldn't find an answer she thought the other woman would accept. The forms were just machines, just moving mannequins. They had no feelings, no intelligence, no needs of their own.

"You'll get used to it," said Dianna, "You'll get to like having the use of them before they get shipped out."

Astrid shook her head.

Dianna grinned. "When you go home tonight, look them up on Internet. Look up the porn. See what it's like. You'll see what I mean."

"There's porn?"

Laughter. "There's porn of everything."

☣

DAY 4

"Arms!" Dianna sang.

Astrid studiously avoided looking over. She'd found the porn. She'd also found her neighbour's history with forms went back several years.

She carefully clicked the muscular arms into place. When she watched what she did, she saw a lifeless, synthetic form. When she tried not to look or blinked or closed her eyes, she felt too soft skin under her hands that brought back images from her research.

"It's just basic physiological response," she muttered, "The body doesn't care that it's tasteless, immoral dross. *You* know better."

She didn't look at the CCTV camera. It had been clear that the footage of Dianna had come from the company's files, even if it weren't admitted. The porn was being used as advertising—even ordinary looking people could take pleasure from copies of famous people.

Astrid thought of the clauses she had agreed to in her employment contract. She'd asked about the request for release of security footage but had accepted the official response. Perhaps the other applicants had been more knowing and aware. Her only experience of forms was watching them through a department store window. She couldn't afford the entry fee for that kind of shop. She had naively thought that all they did was what she'd seen in the windows: prowling, smiling, posing.

Last night's research had disabused her. She'd found a handful of soundless, grainier footage of shoppers. Enough to know that some people emulated the advertising. It was just like any other porn Astrid had seen. One party satisfied, the other there simply to serve and satisfy the others' wants.

Astrid touched dry, soft lips, parting them slightly to show pseudo-mouth behind—then took her hand away abruptly, wiping it on her hip.

☣

DAY 5

"Legs!" Dianna sang, "And we're almost there!"

Astrid got on with her own form. It took a while to get the legs to click into place and he remained sat on the bench while diagnostics ran, servos bending and stretching his legs, the pseudo-muscles and skin flexing as if it were a real, biological body. The head stared blankly, the features frozen.

There was nothing in there. Nothing alive, nothing that thought for itself. A pared down version of the original's personality would be downloaded into the form next week and she would baby-sit for a hundred and twenty hours—five days straight—while the programs settled down.

She'd be allowed to sleep, and eat, and drink, and toilet, but it would all be here, closed off behind opaque glass partitions. Her stomach churned as she realised just what must be going on in those two private workshops.

"It doesn't have to happen," she said to herself, "I don't have to do this. He doesn't have to do this."

Later, she said, "I'll quit," knowing that today would be her last chance because she wouldn't be allowed to leave while the personality was there.

She watched the two opaque workshops become clear, the partitions pulled back, the occupants revealed. The naked, almost sexless forms came to stand in the middle of each workshop. The technicians smiled and laughed. A suited manager arrived.

Astrid hesitated. Surely the personality would put enough on the chips and processors and data storage held in the form that he could decide what he wanted for himself?

※

DAY 6

Astrid returned from the weekend armed with games, books, films and knowledge. She had researched the original as much as she could. There was something about his playful public persona, the way he smiled at the camera, his willingness to be seen with a range of women, that had her convinced it would never tell her anything about the real man. While she suspected she would never like the original, she had an admiration for his apparent awareness of self and social environment. She hoped she could instil something of it in her charge. She might never have been the world's greatest teacher but she flattered herself she'd had some success teaching teenagers to think, not just follow their hormones. And what were hormones but biological programs?

Her heart beat fit to burst as she started the company software.

"Start personality download?" it asked.

Astrid worked a suddenly dry mouth, swallowed a couple of times and, finally, agreed. The workshop drew its partitions, the glass turning opaque as it closed her in. She watched with wide eyes.

It was something of an anticlimax to find that the download and the automatic diagnostic session would take the next twenty-four hours.

※

DAY 7

She woke suddenly. She couldn't have said what woke her, at least at first. Then she realised that strange sensation was the feeling of being watched. She sprung, or tried, from the fold-up single bed. The hammocky bed didn't seem to want to let her go, though, and it took several attempts. She wondered sourly how her neighbour managed to get any kind of performance on this furniture.

"Good morning," she said with a polite smile, the same sort she had always pinned to her face at the beginning of a lesson.

The form sat on the bench and looked at her. There was nothing to say there was life behind the metal eyes. There was no cocked head, no blink, but those were the expected reactions of a child or an animal, not a machine.

"It's polite to let people know you've heard them," she said.

The form said nothing but the fake eyelids almost fluttered, not quite closing into a proper blink. Astrid wiped the sleep from her eyes as she stepped up to the console. There were a series of questions for the first day along with bites of information that should, apparently, be covered so that the form would be familiar with human society.

She reached for the steaming cup of coffee that had appeared in the nearby dispenser and paused.

"Oh."

The form's head pivoted to look at her, a too smooth, mechanical move.

"You were trying to copy what I did, weren't you?"

The question wasn't one on the recommended list, although that probably wasn't why the form didn't respond.

"You tried to blink."

She stood squarely in front of the form and waited for the head to track back to her in another too smooth turn. Then she blinked slowly and deliberately. The form blinked back.

She smiled. "Well done."

The console beeped. A glance showed the first question had been highlighted. With the form still connected up for diagnostic purposes, the company software must be able to track their interactions—and it was demanding that procedure be followed.

"Hello," she said, "I'm Astrid Lee. Who are you?"

"I am a copy of—"

Astrid tuned out the response, watching the console. The words weren't important. It was enough to know that the form was responding as expected.

"You know what you are, then?"

"I am a form, a machine copy of—"

Astrid waved her hand. The response was as required and she didn't need more words to know the form was responding as expected. She saw movement out of the corner of her eye. The form had turned to look at her again. It blinked.

"Am I doing something wrong?"

"No," she said.

"Don't you like me?"

She flushed, caught by features showing an innocence the original probably hadn't known in a long time.

"It's not that," she said, "I just know that you're answering as expected. I don't see much point making you say the same thing again."

"You ask questions you don't want to hear the answer to?"

There was no harm in telling him how things were, if he knew he was a copy. Astrid smiled to soften the blow. "The company software has prompts I have to put to you, to make sure everything has taken properly. You've already said enough for me to know you know, without you saying the whole answer."

The form blinked and then mimicked her smile. It was uncertain and unpractised.

☣

DAY 8

"Good morning, Astrid." The form smiled at her, cross-legged on the bench.

"Mornings are not good," she said.

The form didn't reply, just smiled and returned to looking at the book he held. It was a sign of how well his adjustment was going that he could do something so… human.

She rose and stretched and rubbed away sleep. She still wore yesterday's clothes under the overalls because she couldn't bear to change without privacy.

"Turn around, please," she said in her best teacher's voice.

He looked up from the book to give her the original's Puckish smile, then shrugged and shuffled himself around on the bench.

Astrid watched the broad naked back for a moment before turning so that the CCTV wouldn't capture her hurriedly dropping the overalls to change her underwear.

"What did you do while I was asleep?"

"I read all the other books," he replied, lifting the one he held to show her over his shoulder.

"All of them?"

She knew she read fast and, without allowing for breaks, she would have taken at least two days to get through what she'd brought with her.

"This 'Shakespeare' you brought with you," he said, "I don't know why you bother with… Him or her?"

There was something about the way he sat, about the way it felt as if all his attention was on her and the book was incidental, about the hint of a smile in the shape of his cheek. He was waiting for a reaction. Teasing or learning? Had he picked it up from her prompting yesterday or from his own programming? Was it something the original would do?

"Him," she said, ignoring the prod.

"Do I have to plug back into the console or can we play a game of chess first?"

She smiled. "Let's see what the computer says."

"It'll say there's work to do," he said as he righted himself on the bench again. He swung his legs, a child-like gesture despite the big, muscular frame.

☣

DAY 9

"Let me," he said as she shut down the Internet browser he had been using overnight and started the company software.

Their fingers touched. An accident, both reaching for the console at the same time. Astrid pulled back from the too soft synthetic skin and blushed. The form tapped in a response to the company software's demands, apparently not noticing—or maybe not caring.

"If you're not careful," she said in an even voice, "They'll keep you here to train your siblings and send me off to your new home."

He looked over his shoulder with that mischievous smile again and she promptly forgot the words she'd been going to add, just as she'd already forgotten to ask him what his Internet reading had been.

"I'm just making sure we don't waste time with all this boring stuff," he said, "I do it faster than you, after all."

She sat down, uncertain whether she liked this... Helpfulness? Overbearing manner?

"We can spend more time talking and playing games instead," he said.

He straightened and turned to face her. If she'd felt like she had his attention before, now she felt like she was the centre of his universe. A very small universe, she reminded herself.

"That's okay, isn't it?"

The face puckered, not as child-like an expression as it might have been the day before or the day before that. Today it was the face of a young man, mature enough to realise it was okay to be wrong and ask for correction.

"It's okay," she said with a smile, "But maybe you should ask if someone wants you to do something before you do it?"

"Even little things like typing on a computer? How about the things people don't know they want? Or the things they're too scared to ask about?"

She looked away. "There are some things you shouldn't do just because someone else wants you to."

She felt him watching her but didn't know how to explain herself.

☣

DAY 10

Astrid woke curled up against the broad chest. His hands stroked her back as she swam back into awareness. She wouldn't have thought the fold-out single bed could hold a man of his size, let alone the two of them.

"What— What are you doing?"

She realised her own hands were stroking the dark, too smooth skin, her hips thrust towards him. She adjusted her position to something more seemly and looked away.

"You had some bad dreams," he said, his hands not stopping their soothing motion.

It was almost natural behaviour, the way he answered the unasked "why" instead of the almost rhetorical "what". Was it from the original's personality, the company software or her teaching?

Astrid pulled away from him and got to her feet.

"You shouldn't," she said.

"Why? Don't you want me to?"

She stepped away. The console was already on, with an Internet browser waiting for a search term to be entered. It wasn't the way she had left it but she was too anxious to be doing something to question what the form had been doing.

"It's not appropriate," she said.

She heard the bed creak as it gave up his weight. There wasn't enough space for there to be more than a heartbeat between the sound and his touch. She wrapped her arms around herself.

"You shouldn't worry so much about 'appropriate'."

His fingers kneaded her shoulders gently.

"I'm employed to—" She paused, uncertain what to call this phase. It could no longer be considered 'baby-sitting'. "Look after you."

It was as immoral as if she had taken a shine to one of her students. Except that she used to laugh at the idea of finding one of her half-formed, teenage students attractive, with their gawky teenage frames and their hormonal minds. It was harder to laugh at the idea of a full-grown man.

"I don't need looking after," he said.

Astrid caught her breath as his hands moved from her shoulders, gently tugging her arms so that they rested by her side instead of clutched around her middle.

"I need company," he said simply, "That's what you're here for."

He tugged at her overalls, unzipping it and pulling it so that it was pushed halfway down her arms, restricting her movement—unless she pulled her arms all the way out. His hands trailed down to her hips and pulled her backwards against his chest, against the bulge she had considered safe and sexless.

She should tell him to stop. She should tell him she didn't want this. He must have safeguards, be programmed to follow instructions. He couldn't do this against her will. Her mouth formed the word "please" but she didn't seem to have the air to say it.

She didn't want him to stop. She shouldn't let him do something just because she wanted it.

She didn't manage to find her voice in time, thoughts lost as the soft, dry mouth met her neck. She closed her eyes so she couldn't see the console or the CCTV.

His hands stroked her front, one rising to cup a breast and the other sinking beneath the overalls. Obedient to the suggestion, she parted her legs for his hand and leant against him. The first, gentle touch sent a ripple through her, surprise that it could feel so… normal. The ripples that followed were enough to have her clutching at his hair and hands as she gasped.

Afterwards, she stroked the hand that still nestled between her legs. It was hard to believe the soft, synthetic skin covered hard metals and rigid plastics instead of muscles and bone. He smiled against her neck and she wanted to say something that captured her sense of wonder.

Through the console, a woman cleared her throat. "Miss Lee. This wasn't what we… expected of you."

He stepped back and, for a moment, Astrid was tempted to whimper and follow his reflected warmth. Instead, she zipped up her overalls and did her best to look calm as she faced the manager.

"Oh?" Astrid asked.

The suited woman smiled. "I guess you have some kinks the personality tests didn't highlight. If we'd known we would have matched you with a form intended for… escort services rather than simple companionship."

"Compani—"

"No matter," the manager said. "You've tripled its asking price just based on the CCTV footage of the last couple of minutes. We've even had bids from some exclusive hotel resorts we've been angling for business from."

Astrid closed her mouth with an audible snap, wincing when she heard it.

"In fact, it's to be sent out early—so you need to run through the final diagnostics set and have it ready within the hour."

The manager's picture was gone by the time Astrid had formed a response. She turned to the form. It looked blank and emotionless, leaving Astrid uncertain whether it could feel anything at all.

"Why? Why did you do it?" she asked and, for the first time, she meant just the words that left her mouth. She just wasn't sure if she was asking him or herself.

The form moved past her and connected himself to the console, selecting the diagnostics tool without her input or instruction.

"You seemed to need a good memory."

She thought of him being at a holiday resort, a slave to keep lonely men and women company, and maybe to give them more than a conversation just so they could have a "good memory". Her experience was nothing special. It was just another one of those memories he was there to make. She felt sick.

"How did you know to—" She stopped, not wanting to put it into words.

He didn't answer. The final diagnostic program had begun and the form was as silent, still and lifeless as the moment the personality had first been downloaded. The search engine was still open in the browser window.

She Called Me Baby

Vylar Kaftan

My mother was born Maria Dana Szczepanski-Sanchez, so it's clear why she legally changed it for her career as a model. She became Maria-Danae, no last name, when she was discovered at age 15. When I was born, she named me Maria-Danae, no last name. That's how it was entered in the birth records. I had no name but hers. This is the way our relationship progressed until I was old enough to know better.

—Excerpted from Chapter 1, "She Called Me Baby," by Baby.

⚕

Kip's face on the phone is bright with excitement. "The book's selling like ice cream cakes in hell, kiddo."

I give a lopsided smile and put my feet up on the plush ottoman. Applesauce sloshes out of my bowl onto my thigh. I lean back in my chair and lick it up with the left half of my tongue. I've just had the right half lengthened another six inches. Today it's rolled up and swollen inside my jaw. Until it heals, I speak through a voice synthesizer against my throat. "I didn't know you could sell ice cream in hell. There's probably rules against it."

"Probably. But the rules go out the window when the place freezes over."

I laugh along with Kip. My tongue twitches a little. "It's good to see you again," I say. Kip's been my agent for ten years now, ever since I've been on my own. He's the best in the business.

"How's your tongue?"

"Healing nicely. My hand mods are doing great too." I lift my right hand to show him the series of segmented metal cords that replace my tendons. I wiggle my fingers at him. "I can already bend my fingers backwards to touch my wrist. And I think the implants are scarring nicely—there's a solid line of keloiding here, don't know if you can see that over the phone—"

"Not really, the connection is bad. The locals tell me this is typical for off-planet calls."

"Did you sign the deal for the zero-gee shoot?"

"Still working on it. The station is resisting. The guy who makes the decision is old. Old enough that he remembers your mother's 'Floating' series she did up here, right when the station was built. I think he's got some sort of loyalty to her."

"She doesn't even model anymore."

"I know," says Kip, and a shadow crosses his face. "Baby, I got another message from your mother."

"I told you, I—"

"Baby," he says sternly, "It's really happening this time. She's dying."

I take a deep breath and set down my applesauce. I fold my arms over my breasts. Buddhist mandalas etched into the curved metal press against the skin of my arms. "Kip, she ruined my life. She controlled me for fifteen years and treated me like property."

Kip gives an ironic smile. "I know, hon. I've read your book. I'm marketing it, remember?"

"I'm serious. I have nothing to say to her."

"Even if she's dying, and she asked to see you?"

"I was never a person to her, Kip! I was just a career move." Kip rarely talks to me about my mother, and I wish this conversation weren't happening. I don't like to think about how he used to be her agent years ago. He quit because of an argument with her—I never found out what it was, but I think it was about me. I hired him as soon as I was free from her.

Kip says, "You share her DNA but not her life. You're your own person. You're not your mother, and she knows that."

I clench my teeth so that I don't lose my temper. My new tongue aches with pressure. "She went to court so that she could have me. It's documented evidence, from her court case, that she wanted to have me so that I would inherit her career when she retired."

"The exact wording was 'I wish for my daughter to be cloned from my DNA, so that I may give her a secure future in every cell of her body.' Your mother was giving you a gift—badly, perhaps, but she meant well. Now, will you go see her as she's dying?"

I sigh. "No. I don't want to see her. I've built my own career, despite her efforts to stop me. I have nothing pleasant to say to that woman."

Kip is silent. The interplanetary connection crackles at us. Finally, he says, "Baby, I've respected you all the time I've known you. I've been with you through everything. I chose to work for you, after the split. Remember how I got you that shoot at Tenochtitlan? Your first one, after you left your mother and got your first bodmods? I'm asking you to trust me, hon. I know about all the stuff she did to you—the age-defying creams, the mandatory modeling lessons, that awful therapist she hired to brainwash you. Your mother screwed a lot of things up, I agree. But what I'm saying is, she's dying. You won't get another chance. Listen to me on this one."

"Kip, I don't—"

His voice breaks a touch as he interrupts. "My dad—he was a military man, single father, back during the Philly uprisings in the thirties. I was a punk kid who protested everything. He and I argued over the police response to the uprisings, and then we argued over how I should live my life, and then I split. Never looked back. Didn't hear about his death until six months ago—three years after it happened. I wasn't even mad at him anymore, not really. I'd just lost track of things. Forgotten."

His expression is calm, but he's blinking a lot. I listen to his story, and speak quietly. "I don't know, Kip. This is my mother we're talking about. You know what she's like."

Kip doesn't seem to have heard me. He's gazing into the distance, at something off-screen. "I work with you because I respect you, Baby. Yeah, the pay's incredible, but that's not what I'm interested in. If I don't respect you... I don't think I can do this."

I stare at him in disbelief. I owe most of my career to Kip. He's not just my agent—he's like a father to me. He cares more about me than my mother ever has. "Are you saying that you'll quit? Quit working for me?"

Kip speaks sharply. "Working for a woman who refuses to see her dying mother? Who's built an entire career based on satirizing her mother's work? Whose best-selling book was inspired by her mother and couldn't have been written without her influence?"

I wince. "You make me sound so heartless. I'm not heartless. Am I?"

"No," he says, more gently. "You're not. That's why you'll go to her."

"Don't tell me what to do, Kip."

"I won't, I just—"

"I'm not going," I say. "Yell at me, quit your job—I don't care. I won't see her."

Kip just looks at me. The screen crackles, filling the silence. I take another bite of applesauce. Finally, he says, "This is exactly why I left your mother."

The words fall between us like rocks. Carefully I lap up the last of the applesauce. I'm glad the voice synthesizer masks my tone of voice. "I can't believe you said that."

His voice is calm. "Baby, hon. Talk to me. What's really going on?"

"I'm frightened," I confess. "Every time I think of her, I feel like a child again. She controlled me for so long. I'm worried that if I see her, she'll figure out a way to manipulate me."

"She won't. You're Baby, and you have your own career, your own look. There's no one like you in the world."

I close my eyes for a minute. My mother's face looms in front of me, just as I last saw her, in court: dark-eyed, angular, a femme-fatale beauty. It's the face I was heading towards, when I left ten years ago— the face that I have tattooed, scarred, and reshaped until it's mine. I open my eyes and force the words out. "I need to do this? You're sure, Kip?"

"I'm sure."

"All right. I'll go."

Kip smiles. "Good for you. Later—I've got an appointment with the director up here." He vanishes. I'm left alone in my library, once again pondering what else I can modify, how else I can look different from my mother.

☣

When my mother's controlling behaviors forced me to run away from home, I was four days shy of my fifteenth birthday. Escaping her wasn't easy. I had to bribe some local maintenance workers to smuggle me out, and one of my underground connections to remove the tracking device from my neck. From there, I made my way to a well-known surgeon specializing in unique body modifications. My first procedure was the rune of transformation scarred into my forehead. My second procedure was triple-pierced nipples. I continued to modify my body over the next three months. I call this series Dagaz, after the rune for Breakthrough.

During this time, I went to court and got Emancipated Minor status. I planned to file for financial support from my mother, but she disowned me instead. In response, I started my next series of modification: Teiwaz (or the Warrior), followed by what's widely considered my masterpiece, the Wyrd series. See Appendix A for pictures.

—*Chapter 6, "She Called Me Baby," by Baby.*

☣

It's a week before I can make time to see my mother, since she lives in southern California and I'm up near Puget Sound. Secretly I'm hoping that she'll die before I can get there, which makes me feel guilty. It's been a long time since I've felt anything except anger towards my mother.

I tried to reach out to her once, about three years ago. Kip doesn't even know about this. It was after the shoot at the Phoenix Botanical Gardens, the one where I embraced a saguaro cactus—famous picture, most people have seen it. They say that in the pictures, I look like I'm miles away from the needles in my flesh.

I wasn't miles away—I was years away. My mother held my hand, and it was my sixth birthday. We walked down the paths in the garden, ignoring the paparazzi who stalked us with powerful zoom lenses. I wore a large floppy hat, a dark shield over my face, and a lightweight UV suit to prevent any damage to my skin. My mother had brought me there because I told her I wanted to see the desert. I remember looking up at her, in her identical outfit, knowing I would be just like her when I grew up. A famous model.

That's what I'm thinking about, in the Phoenix series. After the shoot, I emailed my mother and asked her if she wanted to do lunch, my treat, anywhere on-planet she liked. She responded by blocking my address. Furious, I blocked hers too, and that was the end of that.

I remember this moment, and my cheeks flush as I step into my waiting vehicle. My driver waits until I have settled in place, and then closes my door. I stare at the streets of West Seattlewood as we go, at the elaborate houses of my neighbors. My mother would probably like it better up here, where it's cooler, but her generation still has a sentimental attachment to southern California. When I reach downtown, the people on buses stare at my car driving past—probably startled to see a private vehicle outside of Seattlewood. I'm glad that they can't see through my tinted windows. I don't want any attention today.

I'm getting out of the car for my private plane when Kip calls me. I hold the phone in front of me and slip the receiver into my ear. The static indicates that he's still off-planet. "Hey, Baby. Just wanted to tell you how glad I am that you decided to go."

I glance around. Tourists stare at me, but I'm used to being recognized everywhere I go. "If she kills me, sell the pictures and donate the money to charity."

He smiles. "Looks like your tongue has healed—that voice box was terrible. Still on schedule for the spine augmentation?"

"Yeah." I'm getting titanium implants in my spine. They'll let me bend at right angles in my back, and compress my torso by about four inches when I want to. It'll involve nanobots reconstructing each disc of my spine. It's my most intense procedure yet.

Kip nods. "Thank God for immune boosters. I don't even want to think how long it would take you to heal otherwise."

I take a deep breath. "I really don't want to do this, Kip."

"I know, Baby, but it's the right thing to do."

"I have nothing to say to her."

"It'll be fine. You can call me if you need to talk."

Thinking about it makes my pulse race. I have no luggage, so I start walking towards my flight. "How're negotiations?"

He pauses. "Not good. They want your mother's permission before they'll let you do a shoot up here. Just as a courtesy to her. They sent her a form."

"Shit!" I check for reactions from the potential eavesdroppers. I shouldn't be having this conversation in public. You never know where the paparazzi have bugged. Or when a civilian is going to sell his story to the tabloids. The last thing I need is a headline reading "Clone's Career in Jeopardy". They love to make up stories about me, but they're even happier when the stories are true.

Kip sighs. "I know."

"She'll never agree."

"That's true. She might deny permission, in which case it's probably hopeless. Or, she may not get to the paperwork before she passes away. In which case, it'll go to the executors of her estate, and it's hard to say what they'd do, and for what price. The director up here might change his mind, or the whole thing might go to court."

"I'm used to that," I mutter. Since I left her, most of the times I've seen my mother were in court. I still remember the expression on her face when they declared me an Emancipated Minor. She stared at me across the room with a mixture of hatred and helplessness. I stared back, forcing myself to look braver than I felt. Cameras snapped everywhere—capturing her face, capturing mine. I grit my teeth at the memory.

"So, looks like we're blocked here, for now," he says. "I'm looking for other opportunities—"

"I'll make her sign it," I say abruptly.

"What?"

I'm feeling reckless as I duck into a bathroom stall for privacy. I never use the phone rooms—they're always bugged. "Why not? I don't have anything to talk to her about. I'll talk about this. I'll get her to sign it—or, if I can't, I'll get her to reject it, so at least the issue is closed and we don't need the lawyers."

Kip's voice is strained. "Baby, this is your dying mother. Now is not the time to confront her about business."

"Our whole relationship has been about business," I snap. "From the moment she decided to make me—*make* me, not have me."

"Stop it, Baby. Put it aside for now."

"*How?* I've always been a thing to her. I'll do it, Kip. I'll get her to sign it somehow. I know how she thinks. I can get her to do it."

Kip blows air over his lower lip. "Fine."

"I'll catch you later."

"This bitterness hurts you more than it hurts her."

"Good-*bye*, Kip."

I end the call and bury my face in my hands. The warmth of my tattooed right palm contrasts with the coolness of the steel-plated left. I wish I hadn't spoken so sharply to Kip—he's just trying to help. I think about calling him back to apologize, but he's invoked my stubborn side. It's a matter of pride now, to get my mother to sign the form.

☣

The thing to understand about my mother is that she was always in control. Always. Some people remember her for her beautiful face, but more people remember her as the woman who spearheaded the pro-cloning movement. *Maria-Danae v. the United Nations* captured the world for a whole year. And my mother—with her lawyers—won over the World Court, and overturned the old human cloning bans. Although she's got some talented lawyers, my mother was the real mastermind behind the scenes. She knew the case she wanted them to make, and that's what they did. She spent years focused on the issue during my childhood, which may partly explain why she was so unprepared for my case against her.

People ask me what it was like to be a celebrity before I was even conceived, to be in the tabloids before I was born. Answer is, I don't know. I wasn't alive yet. But my whole life was lived as Maria-Danae's clone, until I was fifteen and attained my freedom. Since then, I've spent my career as a model and artist redefining what it means to be Maria-Danae—what it means to be me, to be Baby. I'm proud of my new fame, because it's mine.

—*Chapter 11, "She Called Me Baby," by Baby.*

☣

I'm standing just outside my mother's bedroom. I was admitted to the house by my mother's caretaker, a small gray woman whose name never quite made it to me. She disappears, mumbling something about my mother preparing to see me. So I'm left alone with the room, and my thoughts.

The strangest thing about being back in my mother's house is that it still has artwork I remember. I walk over to an abstract work I used to love when I was a kid. It's blue and purple swirls, which I've always thought looked like a pair of dancing snails. My mother told me it was a stylized yin-yang symbol, with each swirl a small part of the other. I never thought so, because there was so much more purple than blue. It was like the purple snail was dancing on top of the blue one, squishing it into the floor. Mother and I used to like the same art, when I was young. I find that I dislike the painting now. It's a meaningless scrawl, like kindergarten fingerpainting. But my mind is sifting through ideas of a purple-and-blue themed shoot, with body paint to accentuate the tribal tattoos on my lower back—maybe with something pressing me down, like barbells or restraints.

I turn towards her bedroom door and try to listen through it. She and her caretaker are speaking quietly. The caretaker opens the door and speaks to me. "Wait." Her eyes flicker over my face for a moment. Then she walks away down the hall, leaving me alone. There's a print from my mother's *Floating* series on the wall, which I try not to look at.

Finally, I hear my mother say, "Enter." The side of my lip curls, and I go in to meet her.

I know she's been ill, but I hadn't understood how badly. My mother reclines in her large wooden canopy bed. She leans against the white pillows, which are so perfectly symmetrical that I know she arranged them. She wraps the plum-colored Chinese silk robe more tightly around her thin body as she stares at me.

I'm caught by her face, which is wasted from the toxic aftereffects of her skin treatments. Mother used plastastica early in her career, before anyone realized that some people suffered a long-term rejection of the material. This was before it was taken off the market, a decade ago. The effects lasted her for years. During my court battles with her, she could have passed for an older sister. But now my mother is paying for it. Her eyes are sagging, and her skin looks like loose tree bark. It's faded from smooth golden brown to dull beige. The effect is surreal against her beautiful black hair, loose around her shoulders.

I find myself wondering whether I might have tried plastastica if I'd been born in my mother's generation. Looking at my mother now is like seeing a mutilated version of myself. The thought triggers a memory: my mother calling me "mutilated" the first time she saw my bodmods. I change my opinion: my mother doesn't look mutilated. She looks destroyed.

The silence is uncomfortable. "Hi," I say, my extended tongue rolling partly out of my mouth. I don't know where else to start. Now that I see her, getting her to sign the contract seems like the most ridiculous plan ever—although I'm less afraid of her than I thought I'd be.

My mother's hands fall back against her sides. Her robe falls open a little bit, and I notice an electrode attached to the skin over her breastbone. I wonder how many nanobots are working in her lungs, keeping capillaries open so that she can breathe. Her eyes rove over my body, examining my bodmods. Her expression is hard to read through her distorted face. "The tongue is new," she observes. "It looks like a lizard."

"I'm proud of it," I snap. The moment of sympathy has passed. It feels like spikes are lifting from my back as I react to her criticism. Maybe I should install spikes with my new spine.

My mother stares at me without saying a word. Finally, she says, "Yes, of course." She looks down at the white quilt and smoothes it with one hand. The action is very slow. I regret my tone of voice, but I can't take it back.

"Are you in much pain?" I ask, as politely as I can.

"Not much. I've got strong medication." She lets her hand fall and looks at me again. "How is your book?"

I'm startled. "Hit the New York Times bestseller list last week. Hoping it'll go to number one."

"Have a seat." She gestures at the edge of the bed.

I pull over a plush green chair and sit down. "Yeah, the book is selling great. The free press from the tabloids isn't hurting. You and I have always been popular with them."

"I'm sorry I haven't read it," she says. "I've been so tired."

"It's all right. I don't expect you to."

"I wanted to."

"You've got other things on your mind."

"The contract they want me to sign."

Of course she's already read it—they sent it last week. "Oh yes," I say. "Well, there'll be plenty of time to look it over later." She looks so fragile, like a doll, not quite real.

She shakes her head and leans back against the pillow. Her eyes focus on my shoulder, where the strap of my tanktop hides the black X of the Gebo rune. "Baby, it's good that you came. I want to say something."

I catch my breath. I don't want a deathbed confession, not now, not yet. I'm not ready for this. "Mother—"

But she just says, "I didn't know what to do. I still don't. I don't know how I could have stopped you from leaving, how I could have kept you close."

Of course. She's still thinking of me as her possession. I expel my breath in an angry burst. "You *couldn't*. There's no way. You don't control me, not the way you did when I was a kid. I know better now."

My mother looks down at the bed. She whispers, "Do you hate me?"

I pause, not wanting to answer the question. "You raised me to be just like you. You dressed me just like you. You told me I'd be an artist and model, just like you."

She lifts her head and challenges me with her eyes. "You *are* an artist and model, aren't you?"

"You didn't let me make my own choices."

My mother sighs. "You told me that's what you wanted. To be just like me, when you grew up."

"Every daughter says that at some point," I say, but I'm remembering the botanical gardens in Phoenix. I wonder if this is a mind game my mother is playing with me, something to make me doubt myself. She's an expert at making me doubt myself.

Her eyes are angry, as she looks at me. "How could I have known? You were my only child. All I knew was what you told me."

I'm uncomfortable. I try to placate her with words. "Look, I don't know that now is the time to talk about this. What's done is done. You obviously did what you thought was best at the time, and it's all over now." I stand up, wanting to be out of there.

"That's not what I wanted to tell you." My mother's voice is like a hammer. I sit down from the impact.

"What, then?" I ask.

My mother is staring at the wall now. "I wanted to tell you about when I was a girl in San Diego." She pauses, and her voice softens. "It was years ago now. When I was a girl, before I knew anything about contracts or politics or anything, I used to play house with friends. We had little rag dolls that we called our babies. They weren't very good dolls, but we loved them. My doll was named Cecily May—Cecily because it was the prettiest name I knew, and May because it was the month that was both spring and summer. I decided that when I had a daughter someday I would name her Cecily May."

I don't know why she's telling me this story. "Well, why didn't you?"

"I forgot," she said simply. "It was a game as a child. And when I had you, I wanted to generate publicity. Because being famous is about publicity. I wanted the best family business to give you. My lawyers and I agreed that our case was strongest if I showed how serious I was.

They said I should give you my name, so I did."

"I wish you hadn't."

"You could have changed it."

I know she's right. I kept my name because it helped with my career. The world already knew me as Baby, and that fame helped me get my career started. But I say, "It's hard to change a name, once given. You get used to it."

"That's true," she says. "So do you hate me? Answer the question. Please."

"No," I say, surprised to realize that it's true.

She smiles, her eyes filled with relief. "You were right, what you said earlier. I did what I thought was best at the time. You have no idea how much I've hurt myself over this question, whether you hated me after everything that happened. All these years, it's chased me around like dogs."

It's like her, to be thinking of herself even now. But I don't resent her. I reach out and take her hand. It's papery and rough. I say, "There's no use hanging onto it all."

She breathes deeply, and her lungs shudder. "Will you stay with me tonight?"

I look at her ruined face. "Yes," I say slowly. "I can stay tonight. Let me make a phone call."

"About the contract—the one where you want to do a parody of the *Floating* series—"

"Never mind that. We can talk about it later."

She smiles and squeezes my hand. "All right. I was very proud of my *Floating* series, you know. It launched my career."

I let go of her hand and step outside the room. The yin-yang painting catches my eye, and I remember why I liked it. Maybe I should model some dance steps instead, when I do the purple-and-blue shoot—something in a soft light. I'm considering the possibilities as I call Kip. When I reach him, he's holding a margarita in one hand. "Baby! How's the visit to your mother?"

"Complicated. But I'm staying here an extra day."

"Good for you, hon. It must be going great."

"Listen, Kip—drop the negotiations. I don't want to do the shoot anymore."

"*What?* But I just got the contract this morning. Your mother signed it and returned it."

"She did?" I'm confused, but starting to see. "Kip, what's the timestamp on that?"

"I don't know." He glances down at something. "Eight this

morning, Pacific Standard. Wait, when did you get there?"

"Noon. Kip, cancel the shoot."

"But—"

"You heard me. I'm not interested in doing it."

He squints at me. "What do I tell these guys?"

"You'll think of something. I need to go. I'll call tomorrow and we'll figure something else out. Somewhere new for me to go."

"Baby—"

I end the call and turn the phone off. I return to the room where my mother rests. She's fallen asleep in the last few minutes. Carefully, I sit on the bed and take her hand. I stay with my mother and watch her sleep. I imagine her floating, in a space all her own.

Millie

Anna Caro

When my father died, I inherited my coffin.

My parents would be horrified to hear me refer to it as such; more so to know I had been doing so jokingly since my mid-twenties. It doesn't even look like a coffin; it's a cedar chest that had been my maternal grandmother's, with carved feet and an inlay of what looks like mahogany. But I've always known what it was.

Though my driverless car has changed my life at home, it's still technically illegal to drive without having passed the test in a regular car, and I don't want to risk getting stopped this far away. I flew here, but I don't know how I'd start explaining the contents of my coffin to the airline. So after we finish cleaning out the house where we grew up, Cal drives me the two days home with it strapped to the back seat of the car.

Neither of us mention the coffin the whole way.

☣

I first found out about it the year the fires came. The bush behind us, where Cal and I played when he could be bothered carrying my support unit strapped to his back, and when our parents let him, crackled red and orange. We could taste the burnt air. The emergency call rained down on us from the helicopter; stay and defend or leave now. We were already loading up the car—or they were; I was sitting, simultaneously scared and excited, in the back seat. Cal and our parents carried down clothes and valuables and the cedar chest which they somehow managed to squeeze in.

"You'd have to be fucking mad," Dad said, as the words *stay and defend* echoed through the air, but our neighbour was already hosing down the wall of his house, and dad yelled him words of good luck as he sped the car away.

Our house was saved, if with a smell that lingered for years, but the northern tip of town was completely gone. Those days changed things in other ways. I asked what was in the box.

My parents gave each other confused, concerned, terrified looks. They held a whole conversation with their eyes—*do we tell her is she ready maybe not yet she has a right to know*. They reached a conclusion. Cal was sent out with ice cream money.

"Sweetie," my father began, perched on the motel room chair. "You know that in most ways you're just like other girls. You're pretty and clever and we love you very much."

Something was happening. I could sense it in the air, like the crackling fire we had left behind.

"But you understand that some things are different?"

"Because of Millie?" I asked.

"Yes, because of Millie. Because… because of how you can't pick things up or touch things."

"When Callum was a baby," my mother said. "We kept some things so we could remember what he was like when he was little. We kept a bit of his hair and the first tooth he lost… Well, once you weren't like you are now. Once you had a body like Callum does… not one that looked like Callum, one that looked like you… and well when you got Millie, we kept…"

I bolted. I made a beeline for the door and… I couldn't open it. Of course I couldn't fucking open it. I couldn't do what a normal kid could have done. I couldn't stumble past the motel units to the unfamiliar streets of an unfamiliar town. They wouldn't drive round for hours as I got colder and tireder until our eventual reunion. I was stuck.

Mum had her arms round me and I just wanted her to let go, to let go. Powerlessness surged. I needed them to get away from me, for me to get away from them. They couldn't tell me things like this when I had no choice but to stay in that room. The world was collapsing.

☣

We sleep overnight night at a distant cousin's house. I laughing—only not quite laughing—persuade Cal to take the spare room. It isn't like I'll feel discomfort on the sofa. Their uneasiness is obvious as they fed us lasagna. I've learned to laugh it off, ask them to put just a little on the plate so I can smell it, and not to worry, but it feels like I've been telling people that every day of my life, and I'm tired of it. I want to be home, home with Beth—and believe it or not, work—and the familiar streets where Millie and I had adapted to every crack, every unevenness of the footpath.

I dream of childhood that night, which could be a reaction to dad's death, four years after mum's, rather than the box we carry in the car, but is linked all the same. I dream of the perfect little girl I became, with the long blonde hair I could wear loose and flowing without it getting caught in paint pots or door hinges, how I never got a rash or chocolate smears on my face, how sometimes my parents would let me become a princess, and with a few buttons my hair would glitter pink and gold, and a long flowing dress with ribbons and tassels and pearls would appear.

Did it matter that I couldn't hold, couldn't touch? Of course it did. Did it bother me I couldn't go anywhere without someone—someone my parents trusted—to carry Millie? Absolutely. Was I unhappy? I don't think so. The things I wanted to do and couldn't were matched, in my mind at least, by those I could that others couldn't. Even when things became more problematic, it was a simple matter of ability, or lack thereof. I understood that there were things I couldn't do, and I became frustrated by that fact, but I had no sense that it ran deeper than that, no sense of anything being off with my identity in any way.

But it is not those frustrations I dream of; but of a world where I could be anyone, anything.

☣

I chose this apartment partly for the small kitchen. You can't get anywhere without one—legal restrictions on landlords or something, and it's not like it does me any harm, but on principle I didn't see why I should pay for something I wasn't going to use. And whilst it has been pointed out to me that I could technically live in a railway station locker, I appreciate space and decoration and possessions every bit as much as anyone else.

For the first three years I was here, it sat empty. Lovers learned that there would be nothing to eat or means to prepare it, and stopped for kebabs or fish and chips between work and my apartment. That changed when I met Beth. Slowly, carefully, but with a sense of persistence, items began to appear. A glass—and she ran the water for half an hour before drinking, because god knows how long it had been sitting in the tank. Then an electric jug, mug, box of tea. A tin of biscuits. Coffee and plunger.

Had I at any point screamed *get that shit out of my kitchen*, I'm sure she'd have obliged. But I was fascinated. This wasn't an act of exclusion, not a taunting of normalisation. This was change, merging, compromise.

She's cooked and is waiting for us. By now the kitchen has grown to functional. Not like hers with lemon zesters and bottling equipment and countless sizes of spoons, but the sort you might find in a student flat—enough to cook meals, if only of a basic sort.

So she serves Cal chicken risotto, and puts a little out for me, and we talk and laugh and for now I don't think about the fact that my body's in the boot of Cal's car, and at some point in this evening Cal and Beth are going to have to walk outside and carry it up in the lift and it's going to be here, with us and Millie and my furniture and photographs.

☣

My first real crush was on a boy. A good thing too, because I'm not sure I could have dealt with any more turmoil at that point in my life. There were others, of course, on girls too, in retrospect, but this was the first one with real strength, the first I really felt, that really shook me. The first that made me realise something was wrong.

His name was Yusuf. He was a year older, but in my class for maths because I'd been pushed ahead. He'd work with me when so many— particularly the boys—were angry at having this girl a year younger than them who could easily outshine them, much less one who—they said—didn't even really exist. I'm not sure whether it would make things better or worse if they knew I was only so good with maths and computers because there were so many things I couldn't spend my time on.

That was when I began to realise something was missing.

It took me almost two years to act on it. I had started insisting on seeing the doctor alone a few months before, so it wasn't new that my mother brought Millie inside and then left to get a coffee. He talked to me about how my projection is moving, did some cognitive tests. He asked if I have anything I want to ask. Usually the answer is no.

Shyly: "We've been learning about... bodies in school. Sex ed."

He frowned. I continued.

"The bodies in the pictures aren't like mine. Can my body be like that. I *am* thirteen now."

"You do know the age of consent is sixteen," he says.

I looked down. "Yes." Embarrassment was pushing up inside me.

"You're still a child. Come back when you're older and we'll look at making you an adult. Believe me, it's better this way."

I left, burning, hoping he wouldn't tell my parents.

Beth stays the night, as she does at least three a week. Sleeping in a bed—actually lying beneath the covers—is something I rarely did before Beth. Now I do it every night, even when I'm on my own. It's a little dubious, even now with all the improvements in projection technology I still sometimes cut across and between the covers, and if Beth were to look she would often find that parts of me were not there.

It doesn't seem to freak her out.

I survey the room before using the infrared capabilities I added to Millie to shut the lights off. I try to shut off all thoughts of my parents, of my old home, to ground myself in the present and ignore the little girl with twisted limbs and no tone in her neck, whose parents decided she would be better off as a brain and a projection, a girl with no body and with the perfect body.

I look round. There's a collection of ceramic snails on the dresser. A painting I bought at a co-workers' daughters' exhibition. A mirror. The drawers are full of Beth's clothes.

Come to bed, Beth says, and I do. I perhaps can't feel her skin as warm, but I know it is.

⚕

Maths was abstract. I enjoyed and was good at it, but the only practical purpose was to prove myself.

What it formed the foundation for, hacking, was the opposite.

I only got my genitals four months before my sixteenth birthday. But those four months were everything to me; the first real control I had over my body.

By my mid twenties, with a post-graduate degree behind me and a software engineering job, I realised there had to be an alternative to relying on a series of care assistants when I could afford them, friends when I couldn't, to assist my every movement. Millie gained wheels and a motor, the ability to move according to messages I sent. For the first time in my life I walked somewhere alone.

It wasn't that I was ashamed of Millie. But one too many encounters with a curious dog, child—or, worse, adult who should have known better, began to terrify me. My whole consciousness was in that projection unit—if she was badly damaged, I died. If she was stolen, I was kidnapped. Only the law didn't see it that way, and most people didn't either. It was time to make her a bit less like a mechanical animal who ran along behind me. A bit less cute. With help from friends, I encased her in a suitcase with wheels and with a bit of practice learned to hold my arm back to give the appearance of dragging her. With a technician on call, automatic doors and other modifications to the apartment, and an occasional cleaner to stop the buildup of dust, I had more independence than anyone could have thought possible.

⚕

It's now or never. It takes about an hour of brain-commanding Millie's movements—which are, after all, amateur built and mostly designed for walking along footpaths—to flip open the lid of the chest with the suitcase handle. I look away, then force myself to look back.

They paid for high quality preservation techniques, and she looks almost alive. A toddler with dark blond hair. You can't even really tell there was anything different about her—her limbs have been manipulated to lie perfectly straight. She could just be sleeping.

Can I say, with all honesty, whether I'd be better with that body? No. I've tallied up the columns in my head before, the way they do when you're deciding whether to get a job or stay in school, whether to buy a car or save for a house deposit. But they're not easy points of comparison; how do you rate being able to touch and hold objects versus the mobility Millie brings me? What is the comparison between feeling constant pain and never knowing this feeling that drives so much of what other people do?

I don't know which choice I'd make, but I want that choice back.

And in some ways I'm almost glad that my parents are gone, because there will never be the temptation to ask them if they were really thinking about the pain I would be in, or the fact my body scared them. To ask if, even subconsciously, there was a hint of revulsion at my limbs and my neck. To ask if this was not about me at all really, but because they'd pictured a little girl before I was born, who could run and jump and catch and that was what they wanted, even if they couldn't touch her.

⚕

When cedar burns, it cracks and pops, even explodes, risking igniting everything in its path. So Beth half carries, half drags, the coffin down the narrow path to this small, isolated bay north-east of the city to the still damp sand. When we get the fire going, it burns hot and crackles against the ripple of the waves.

This isn't a perfect solution, because we live in a world where people make imperfect decisions for imperfect reasons. But it is my decision, and this is what I need to do.

Beth leans closer to me. There's space for her.

Frankenstein Unraveled

Lori Selke

Frankenstein's monster was doing his morning calisthenics when he felt a small but palpable pop, just under his ribcage, on the left. It didn't hurt, exactly, but it was uncomfortable enough that he went to check it in the mirror.

Morning calisthenics were a crucial portion of the self-care routine of Frankenstein's monster. If neglected, his limbs tended to stiffen up in a facsimile of rigor mortis. It was annoying but understandable, considering.

He plodded to the bathroom and pulled up the thin cotton undershirt he wore. Scars both thick and thin, white and vivid red traced their jagged paths along his torso. Here and there thick ridges of skin were joined together with a series of stout black sutured X's. And there, yes, just below the seventh rib, he could see the short frayed end of a loose thread. Clear lymph oozed slowly out of the gap left by the broken stitch. Frank dabbed at it with the hem of his undershirt.

The bandage called itself "flesh-colored" but the shade of the adhesive plastic did not match the skin tones on either side of the broken stitching; above the rib Frank's skin was pale and sprinkled with cinnamon-colored freckles, while below incision his skin had a sallow, mushroomy cast to it. Fortunately, no-one would see it once he put a clean shirt on.

The popped stitch continued to ooze fluid throughout the day. By the evening, the edges of the original incision had begun to turn pink and tender to the touch. Frankenstein's monster was worried about infection. He rubbed an over-the-counter cream into his sundered flesh and covered it with a clean square of gauze.

In the morning, the gauze was mottled with brownish stains. Frankenstein's monster decided to see a doctor.

☣

The waiting room smelled strongly of tongue depressors. There was a rack of pamphlets on one wall, a large flat-screen television on another. The floor was carpeted in a neutral pattern that neatly disguised whether or not it had been cleaned recently. The plastic chairs were uncomfortably narrow on Frankenstein's monster's hips, and, tall as he was, they provided very little support for his back.

The front reception desk was made of curved blonde wood. The woman behind the desk wore scrubs with a pattern made of smiling angel children holding rainbows. Her hair was straightened and pulled back into a no-nonsense ponytail. She barely glanced at him as she asked him to sign in, then handed him a clipboard full of paperwork.

There were five names ahead of him on the sign-in sheet, but only three other people sitting in the waiting area. One man in coveralls coughed into a bandana every few minutes. One woman sat with her young son in her lap. Her son was playing an electronic game of some sort, but his mother was watching the big-screen TV. An older, heavyset woman slept in a chair in the corner; Frankenstein's monster could hear her snoring lightly.

Frankenstein's monster sat with his knees drawn up near his chest, carefully balancing the clipboard with its thick sheaf of paperwork. He read the opening paragraph of the three-page form labeled Adult Medical History three times. "Your answers on this form will help your clinician understand your medical concerns and conditions better. If you are uncomfortable with any question, do not answer it. Best estimates are fine if you cannot remember specific details. Thank you!" First, the boxes: Current medications, allergies, surgical histories. Then the checklists: has any member of your family had any of the following conditions? Asthma. Anemia. Cancer, Breast. Cancer, Colon. Cancer, Melanoma. Cancer, Skin (except melanoma). Depression. Diabetes. Eczema. Glaucoma. Mental Retardation. Mitral Valve Prolapse. Osteoporosis. Tuberculosis. Do you smoke? Do you drink alcohol? Have you ever used needles? Have you been immunized for the following—please list month and year. Are you interested in being screened for sexually transmitted diseases? Do you use a seatbelt? Please check any current problems or conditions you are experiencing on the list below. Fevers/chills/sweats. Chest pain/discomfort. Nausea/vomiting/diarrhea. Discharge: penis or vagina. Rash. Cough/wheeze/difficulty breathing. Anxiety/stress.

His pen hesitated above each gray square. In the end, he left the entire form blank.

The television was playing a news story about a man who had lost his leg in an accident. The man had his amputated leg embalmed so that it could be buried with him when he died. He stored the leg in a storage locker. When he fell behind in rent, the storage company auctioned off the contents of his unit to another local man, who planned to use it in a Halloween haunted house display. Who owns the leg? asked the newsreader. After all, hadn't the buyer purchased it fair and square? But could an embalmed limb ever be simple property? Who had the rights? That may ultimately be for the courts to decide, the journalist with the bland face and the perfect brown hair intoned solemnly, staring sincerely at the camera before glancing down at the papers on his desk.

Next: weather and sports.

After an hour and a half of waiting, the woman at the front desk called his name and ushered him around the corner into a small cubicle. Another woman, broad-shouldered and heavy around the hips, took the clipboard from him as she sat down. She glanced at the first page.

"Mr. Frank Lux?" She pronounced his last name like "lucks." He nodded. "You have some torn stitches on your left side, is that correct?" She started typing into a desktop computer, glancing across her shoulder as she spoke. Frankenstein's monster grunted assent. "You've recently had surgery?"

Frank cleared his throat. "No. These are old stitches."

The woman stopped typing for a moment and turned to look at him. Then she typed a short burst of characters into her computer. Her next question was, "can I see your wrist, please?"

Frankenstein's monster extended his arm, palm up, exposing yet another trail of thick black stitching. The woman picked up a handheld scanner from her desktop and waved it over his forearm. She paused, glanced at her computer screen, and then waved it again. Another burst of typing followed and then she turned to look at him.

"I'm sorry, sir, but the scanner seems to have an error. The DNA scan is giving me two different IDs." She reached over and ruffled through the paperwork he had just filled out, stopping to peer at the three blank pages of medical history. "Sir?" she said again.

"I don't have insurance," Frankenstein's monster rasped.

"Sir, we're happy to treat uninsured patients for a reasonable fee. But if you do carry insurance, we're required to bill your carrier for services. Now, my records are showing here that you have two different carriers. Can you tell me which one I should bill?"

Frankenstein's monster stared at his wrist, the puckered skin stretched over the fine bones, the veins ropy and blue. After a moment, the woman reached out her own hand and placed it gently over his. "I'll tell you what," she said. "I'll make a note in the file here that you paid your co-pay and I'll take care of the billing this time. This is your current address and phone number, Mr. Lux?"

He nodded.

"OK. Please take a seat in the lobby and the nurse practitioner will see you shortly."

☣

The nurse practitioner, tall and slim and nut-brown and wearing a startlingly white lab coat, surveyed Frank's gash through the slit in his paper gown. There were small but deep creases along her brow line as she ran the tips of her manicured fingers lightly along his skin.

He sat under white fluorescent light in a tiny curtained alcove, perched on the edge of a folding metal bed. His work shirt sat neatly folded in a chair next to the bed. The nurse practitioner did not sit down. She wore heavy black shoes, he noticed. Clogs. They made her bare, knobbed ankles look somehow fragile. The hem of her dress, or skirt, or whatever she wore, was shorter than the hem of her spotless coat. He could see the way her spine dipped between her shoulder blades as she bent to examine him. He tried to stare past her curved back to the speckled and scrubbed linoleum floor beyond the curtain's edge before shifting his gaze upward, to the acoustically pitted ceiling. One was shiny, one was flat. One was arranged in squares, the other in rectangles. But they both shared the same industrial off-white shading, the same random flecks of black. Floor. Ceiling. Ceiling. Floor. He tried not to tense or flinch when she touched him. Shouldn't she be wearing gloves? Powder blue or latex-beige? Or purple, or perhaps even black? He felt a shiver run through his skin. He hoped the electrical waves of sensation and tension weren't visible to the naked eye.

"I don't want to sew up that incision until the infection has receded," she said in the general direction of his abdominal area before standing upright again. Frankenstein's monster hunched his shoulders so that she could look down at him. "You don't have any allergies, do you?" she asked. Frank grunted. She scribbled on a small pad attached to her clipboard, tore off the page and handed it to him. "Take the antibiotics twice a day for a week. Make sure you take all the pills, OK? You need to finish the entire course of medication even if you start feeling better right away. If you don't see any change in a day or two, come back to the clinic." She wrote a short note on another page on her clipboard. "I'm also going to give you a referral to get that incision taken care of for good. That way you don't have to come back to the clinic." She handed him a larger piece of paper, a form on letterhead. Then she swept through the blue check curtains as quickly as she had arrived.

☣

The incision area was no longer hot, pink and swollen. It had receded to a grayish color on one side and a more tawny shade on the other. But Frank had also lost several more stitches, exposing an ugly, crusty red littoral between the dried and rounded scar tissue bluffs of his skin.

Carefully, with blunt, fleshy fingertips, he poked out the number of the referral the clinic had given him onto the touch pad of his phone.

He listened to the mechanical jingle of the phone ringing, once, twice, three times. A click and a pillowy pause. A computer-generated voice enunciated in his ear, telling him the name of the clinic, the street address and phone number, and the daily office hours. He was calling well within the articulated parameters. "Please stay on the line," the voice reassured, "and your call will be answered in the order in which it was received. If you would prefer to leave a message in our voice mail box, please press the pound key." Then silence. Frank did not push the key. "Please hold." And then a melody that he vaguely recognized from shopping malls and coffee shops played over the line. He waited, holding the phone to his ear, until his shoulder started to ache. Then he set down the phone on the table and pushed the orange button for speakerphone. The room filled with pleasantly melodic pop hooks.

Ten minutes later, the music dropped out and the computer-generated voice returned, smoothly intoning, "We're sorry. All lines are busy. Please leave a message after the tone and we will return your call as soon as possible."

☣

The next day, Frankenstein's monster tried again. He chose a different hour of the day, earlier this time. He dialed the same number as before, carefully double-checking each digit against the piece of paper the clinic had provided him. The same computerized voice answered, and provided the same information as before. A different vaguely recognizable melody played while he waited.

This time he stayed on hold for only five minutes.

"Hello, Wound Care Center of Lake Geneva, how may I help you?"

Frankenstein blinked. "I thought," he hesitated. "This was the number for the Wound Care Center of Hamline?"

"Yes, we sometimes answer their phones for them when they're busy. How may I help you?"

Frank cleared his throat. "I have a referral. I need to make an appointment."

"Can I have your name, please?"

"Frank. Frank Lux."

"And the reason you wish to make an appointment?"

"I need some wound care."

"Can you identify the problem area?"

"My rib cage. On the left."

"Thank you." Frank could hear the sound of papers shuffling in the background. "I'm sorry, Mr. Lux, but I don't appear to have your referral on file."

"I have a copy, here with me." Frank's words were halting and slow.

"Could you fax it over to us or have your doctor fax it to us, please? I'm afraid I am unable to make an appointment without a referral."

"I don't have a fax machine."

"Can you get your doctor to fax it to us?" came the reply.

"I don't have a doctor. The referral is from the urgent care clinic."

"Can you call the urgent care clinic?"

In a small voice, Frankenstein's monster asked, "Can't you?"

"Sir, I'm sorry, I need the referral form before I can process this any further for you."

"OK. I understand." Frankenstein's monster hung up the phone.

The next day he called the urgent care clinic and left a message on their voice mail system to fax the referral to the wound care center in Hamline. In the meantime Frankenstein's monster covered the unraveling ends of his stitches with a large gauze pad, awkwardly secured with lengths of medical tape. At the end of the day, the tape left bright red patches on his skin. The patches itched. He spread a cream on them at night.

Two days later the urgent care clinic called him back.

"Mr. Frank Lux?" the voice on the other end of the line asked. She did not possess the smooth tones of the computer-generated woman. She broadened her vowels, and there was a distinct twang to her R's.

"Yes, this is Lux."

"Mr. Lux, you visited our clinic recently and were given a referral to a wound care center, is that correct?"

"That is correct."

"Did you want to visit the center in Lake Geneva or in Hamline?"

"I would prefer the center in Hamline."

"OK." The voice drew out the phonemes, consonants and vowels both. "Because the referral was for Hamline, but the center in Geneva is the one that called us."

Frankenstein's monster swallowed. He formed his words carefully and slowly. "I called the number for Hamline, but I was transferred to the center in Lake Geneva."

"I see. Hold on."

A click, and dead air. Frankenstein's monster continued to hold the phone to his ear.

Five minutes. Six. Seven. At eight and a half minutes, another click.

"Are you still there, sir?"

"Yes, this is Lux."

"All right. I've spoken to the wound center in Hamline and I will be faxing over another copy of your referral shortly. They should call you in the next day or two. If you don't hear from them, call me back, all right? My name's Nichole, ask for Nichole."

"Nichole," Frankenstein's monster repeated. "Thank you."

He hung up the phone.

⚕

Two days later, the phone rang. Frankenstein's monster checked the caller ID. It was the wound care center in Hamline. He pushed the green button on his phone.

"Lux here," he said.

"Mr. Lux? This is the Hamline Wound Care Center. I hear you've been having difficulties reaching us? I want to apologize."

"Thank you," Frankenstein's monster said.

"I am so sorry about any confusion. My name is Nichelle, and if you have any problems in the future, please just ask for Nichelle. I see some notes on your file here that you tried to make an appointment before but we didn't have a copy of the referral, is that correct?"

"Yes," said Frankenstein's monster.

"Well, now I have a copy of the referral in your file so we can get started." Nichelle's voice was so warm, like buttered bread. Tears began to gather at the corners of his eyes.

⚕

A week later Frankenstein's monster entered the lobby of the Hamline Wound Care Center. The plaster walls of the Wound Center were painted in a soothing shade of honeydew. The short pile carpet was decorated in an abstract pattern of green and black dots, splashed with white. Everything was very clean and in perfect repair. The white faux-leather chairs curve like a hug. The complimentary magazines were laid out in a perfect fan upon the scratch-free glass table.

Frankenstein's monster checked in with the receptionist, a young woman with her sleek black hair tied in a knot at the nape of her neck, just above her stiff white collar. She had a wide smile for him. "Welcome, Mr. Lux." She handed him a clipboard, thick with paperwork. Then she held up the too-familiar device, his nemesis, the hand-held DNA scanner. She gestured for his wrist with her hand. She had rhinestones on each lavender nail.

Reluctantly, knowing what was to come, Frankenstein's monster rolled up his sleeve and extended his arm. He held his breath. The red bars of light flickered across his skin.

The receptionist looked at her computer screen and then looked at Frank. She glanced at his wrist, thick with stitching. "Mr. Lux..." she began.

He opened his mouth to speak, to explain. He turned toward the blonde wood door of the Wound Center, ready to leave. The receptionist continued. "There seems to be a problem with your insurance," she said, peering at the screen. "It could be my error. This scanner acts up sometimes. I'll sort it out while the doctor looks at you, is that all right?"

Frankenstein's monster nodded.

"Please have a seat and the doctor will be with you in a moment."

Frankenstein's monster squeezed his body into one of the leatherette chairs. The cushions hugged his hips and thighs. He balanced the clipboard on his knee. He had finished only the first page when the doctor called his name.

"Mr. Lux? I'm Dr. Vals." She stood in the hallway that led to the examination room. He lumbered up to shake her hand.

She led him down a hallway full of closed doors interspersed with giant photographic prints. The prints showed botanical specimens in great detail, suffused with light within and without. Ginkgo, fern, Japanese maple. Some were tinted green; they match the carpet. Others were yellowish-brown, for subtle contrast. Some were almost silver, colorless.

The examination room was at the end of the hall. It was surprisingly large, with room enough for a desk and a counter as well as a medical table. The square of pastel yellow paper waited for him, neatly folded on the table top. "You only have to take off your top, Mr. Lux," the doctor said. "I'll give you some privacy and be back in a few minutes. Take your time." And she shut the door behind him soundlessly.

Several long minutes later she returned, donned a pale blue pair of medical gloves, and carefully peeled down the front of Frank's gown. She peered at his unraveling incision. "It's not tender to the touch, correct?" She asked. Her voice had changed timbre from perky and warm to cool and clinical. Frankenstein's monster nodded.

"And this has been affecting you for...?"

"About a month."

The doctor nodded. She touched one fingertip to the exposed black end of his stitching. "Can I ask you why you still have all these stitches in place?" She said. "They should have come out a long time ago."

Frankenstein's monster hunched his shoulders. He hesitated before responding. "I think he expected me to return for further... treatment," he finished. The doctor simply nodded again.

"Well, the infection seems to have cleared up, so that's good. I can fix this up for you easily, but it appears that you have a lot of these temporary stitches?" She looked him up and down with a swift, professional glance. The tracks of black X's were exposed on his arms, over his chest, along his jaw and hairline. Frankenstein's monster imagined them throbbing, glowing underneath his paper gown, shining their unearthly light through his threadbare clothing.

The doctor had already busied herself with wiping down the edges of his wound with alcohol pads, then a topical numbing agent. "I'm just going to put a few dissolving sutures in here," she said as she sewed. "Just in case you can't get back to the clinic again in a timely fashion." She looked over the black frames of her glasses at him for a moment before returning to work. "But if you experience any irritation or allergic reaction—red skin, rashes, itching—I want you to come back as soon as possible. Also, you should know that these sutures are more likely to leave some scarring in their place. I figure here on your abdomen, that's not such a big concern." Frankenstein's monster felt her tug once, twice, and then knot the final suture thread. She stood up and took a step back.

"There! That was easy." She smiled at him before her expression took a concerned turn. "But ideally I would like to set up a treatment plan for you to get the rest of those sutures removed and replaced. Because really, sutures like these are supposed to be a short-term solution," she said. "We want to avoid complications from the stitches pulling on your skin. In some ways, you're lucky that in this case the stitching simply broke and began to unravel, although," the doctor frowned, "I don't know why your surgeon used a running stitch instead of an interrupted stitch here."

"He was an eccentric," Frankenstein's monster said.

"I had gotten that impression," the doctor replied. "So, with your cooperation, why don't we bring you back in about once a week for the next six weeks? We'll see if your insurance will cover that, OK?"

"Um," Frankenstein's monster said.

Frankenstein's monster stood once more before the receptionist with the sleek black bun. "So you need six more weeks?" she said, peering at the form in front of her. "If we can untangle this insurance problem, that is."

Frank held his breath.

"The problem I see here is that your DNA scan brought up two different insurance policies. Are you covered by more than one insurance plan, Mr. Lux?"

"I don't know," Frankenstein's monster replied.

"It's OK, it's not illegal or anything," the receptionist said. "It can cause some bureaucratic headaches, but that's why they pay me the big bucks." She flashed him a brilliant smile. "I can bill both companies and see what they're willing to cover and what we can cobble together for you. And then we'll just bill you for whatever they don't cover. Does that work for you, Mr. Lux?"

"I suppose," said Frankenstein's monster.

"Good. I'll go ahead and schedule your appointments, then. Oh, one more thing, Mr. Lux? Do you have any previous names on file I should be aware of? When I run these insurance policies through the computer, I keep getting different names. It's very confusing."

☣

Frankenstein's monster stood in line at the library, clutching his books to his chest.

"Paper, eh? You're old-schooling it," said the librarian. She was clearly in a good mood. Her hair was bound up into dozens of of tiny neat twists; some were shot through with gray. Her dark brown lipstick matched her nails.

Frankenstein's monster grunted and placed his books on the slate-blue counter. The librarian waved the scanner across their spines.

"Thinking of running off to the Great White North?" she said, gesturing at the travel guide to Canada in the pile. Frankenstein's monster looked up, startled. "Let me guess." She touched the cover of Home Wound Care lightly. "Fleeing the country for the promise of political utopia and socialized medicine." She leaned across her desk as she pushed the books back to Frank. "Listen. Take my word as an old lady who's seen it all. Canada ain't all it's cracked up to be. They're trying to turn their system into ours, to save money they say. And it looks like they'll succeed." Besides, she added as she handed back his library card, "They'll shoot you before you ever make it across the wall. Canada's great for tourism but these days, you wouldn't want to live there even if they'd let you."

"I've always liked the cold," Frankenstein's monster said.

"Well then enjoy your vacation," the librarian replied with a wink.

☣

Frankenstein's monster sat in curved white faux-leather chair, surrounded by melon-colored walls, his feet on the speckled carpet. He balanced a clipboard thick with paperwork on his knee. The papers all asked the familiar questions. Name. Address. Insurance. Medical history. Family medical history. Frankenstein's monster had brought in a print-out of his own narrative account of why he couldn't answer these questions, how he had acquired his sutures and why they had never been removed. He wasn't convinced his doctor would ever read it, but for now it, too, was attached to the clipboard, straining the metal jaws at the top. His pen, a ballpoint with blue ink that he'd borrowed from the receptionist, was starting to skip. He bore down hard as he completed the section marked "Please review the following and check any current symptoms that pertain to you." He tried not to think of the medical bills that might well be winging their way toward his home this very moment. Or perhaps they would be waiting with a warrant for his arrest on insurance fraud when he tried to return to his modest apartment. Or maybe he would be lucky and would discover that Victor had used a live donor for his hand or his forearm, in which case a man somewhere across the country might have to field a strange phone call from an insurance auditor. Or even better, the man might simply sigh and sign the bill. Frankenstein's monster hoped he was right-handed; hoped that if not, that prosthetics technology really had advanced as far as they claimed.

The ballpoint pen skipped again. Frankenstein's monster tried to restart the ink by scribbling swirls in the white margins of the paper. He scratched and he scratched, and as he worked he heard a sickeningly familiar "pop."

He turned over his wrist. Thick black stitches that wound around like a bracelet, each X a link in the chain. One of the links had broken. The ends of the thread poked out, exposed. The flesh underneath was beading up with a thick, clear liquid.

Frankenstein's monster stared at his sundered flesh for a moment— short or long, he didn't know. His ears crashed with the sounds of blood rushing through his veins. He could see nothing else but the broken black X, the moles and freckles marring his sallow skin, the traces of blue and green rivers beneath, like a pirate's map. X marks the spot. Dig here. Buried treasure. He stood up and asked the receptionist for another pen.

Her Bones, Those of the Dead

Tracie Welser

The first stage was not a big deal, she just had to give up her body temporarily. She wasn't fond of it anyway, big-boned under her uniform, swollen around the breasts and hips, and puffy in the uncovered places around her eyelids. Sarah stepped into the upright unit, closed the plastic door and then the bulging, sagging self she disliked vanished. Electrical impulses flowed through her and the world inside the uploader unit, and the habitat fell away, replaced by violet skies, dim sun on the horizon, rocky wasted landscape, and mechanized arms. Her own arms, flabby in low-G, were replaced by a powerful new body that towered three hundred feet tall. Her stride covered hills and twisted, stationary lifeforms that passed for trees. Fluttering somethings circled the monolith Sarah became, a form she inhabited comfortably with a mechanical sigh, her former self shed like the discarded carapace of an insect.

"Engage primary drill in sector five-eight-three grid," came the soft voice of the Controller, a reminder of the task at hand, the price of her scenic escape. With the barest hint of effort, she swiveled in the mech and in four broad strides reached the excavation site. Three other mechs drilled at pre-selected locations, while another, the loader, labored to remove rubble that was formed by the drills to the sorting site.

She engaged the drill attached to the mech arm, and worked in silence, as always. Fragments of rock, some weighing several tons, flew in all directions, but no sound penetrated her quiet refuge. Other than an occasional mechanical echo of her own heartbeat or breath, she had no reminders that she was not really walking on planet Earth at all.

It was the end of the shift, the return of her senses to her body aboard the orbiting craft, that Sarah dreaded.

A hiss and a pop, and then the white door slid open.

"Why can I hear my breathing, in the mech?" she asked Tech A-5. Cool metal hands unstrapped clamps and confirmed her vitals before the tech answered.

"You are experiencing sensations related to the maintenance of your physical body," the robot said in lilting monotones. "Involuntary response." A cool light flickered over her torso as it scanned the identification badge on the shoulder of her gray uniform. "Sarah, you are, after all, still human."

"But I don't want to hear my breath," she said. "I like the quiet of the mech, on the surface."

"Perhaps you should apply for stage two," Tech A-5 said.

In the orbiting habitat's corridor, bodies with masked faces jostled against her, straining and bumping their separate ways through to work shifts, or to cramped rooms where dispensers doled out plastic boxes of unappetizing colored foodstuffs synthesized from reclaimed waste product and proteins. She exhaled as the door of her tiny room slid home behind her. Laughter from an adjacent room broadcast clearly through the walls.

"Another thrilling evening," she said without humor, and pulled out the long drawer that contained her sleeper unit. She flopped down without removing her boots or mask, and the bed creaked in protest. "Where's Lindsey?" she asked.

"Lindsey is in the recreation suite," the smooth voice of the Controller said over the interconsole.

"How many others are there?"

"Two individuals currently occupy the recreation suite."

"Good." After a moment, she stood up. "Maybe I'll go up there."

"This is your sleep interval, Sarah," said the Controller.

"I'd rather go to the rec suite," Sarah said, and stepped in front of the door.

It did not slide open.

"Controller, please open the door."

"That request is not recommended," said the Controller.

"Balls," said Sarah. Sighing, the plump young woman with mousy brown hair slid back down onto the bed and pulled off her mask. She slept with her boots on. She faced the wall and dreamed of open skies.

☣

"Before Earth was used up, people lived and worked on the surface," the teacher said.

"Balls," said the little girl in the front of the circle. "My sire said there's nothing down there but rocks and dust!" The other children gathered at the teacher's feet tittered.

"Sarah, you are speaking crudely," said the teacher, "not to mention out of turn. You will observe." The man, Samuel, touched the dark display screen beside him, and it lit up. The image elicited gasps from tiny mouths all around the circle of students, who until then had only seen the planet below through port windows.

"A barren place, with no life other than a few mutated species with little caloric value," said Samuel. "But once it was lush with plant life, and animal, too." A series of scenes followed, depicting unfamiliar shapes and combinations of color: bright greens like a variegated rug against blues and golds resembling hues seen only in paint pots, populated by creatures whose intelligent eyes ennobled human-like but oddly patterned faces.

"Big teeth," said a wide-eyed cherub-boy, finger firmly up his left nostril.

"What's that box, right there?" the girl asked, jumping up to gesture, as well as block the screen from view.

"Sarah!" said the teacher in sharp tones. "That's three marks against you. Remove yourself to the Discipline Room." A breathless pause, and a dozen pairs of youthful eyes watched Sarah as she walked, head held high in her tiny blue jumpsuit, through the door of the nursery. The white plastic door *snicked* shut behind her.

"This, children, is a house," Samuel said. "People once lived on the surface in structures such as this."

☣

The smack of her fist into the boy's face was satisfying. A moment of rare pleasure slowly unfolded, and she observed his hazel eyes turning back in his pale, pimpled face as he slid up the bulkhead of the airlock, mask askew, and tumbled ankles over shoulders in the zero G. His head bumped against the wall.

Dimly, her awareness registered the clamor of the warning siren. Sarah floated a few feet above the floor and treaded the air as she was propelled gently backward by the force of her punch. She made her way to the access panel of the airlock, swimming through the empty space, and hesitated a moment, her finger on the button. She savored the silence, the small but free quiet of the airlock.

The boy moaned.

Sarah squeezed her eyes shut and pressed the button. Low G returned, and her feet touched down just as the boy's prone body thumped, eliciting a louder groan.

The white inner door clanked open, and a maintenance unit waited on the other side, with a discipline unit on the approach.

"The airlock is fully functional," said the maintenance bot. It detached its data cord from the outer access panel, and the alarm ceased. "User error is the likely cause of disturbance."

"Brilliant deduction," she said, arms folded, but the bot was not addressing her.

The discipline bot rolled forward, its antennae swiveling toward the girl. It scanned her ID badge.

"Sarah," it said. "You do not have prior authorized access to this airlock. The absence of your biocontaminant-prevention mask also violates dress regulation."

"It's right here!" Sarah said, punctuating her reply with a shake of the torn mask in her hand.

"You will accompany me to the Discipline Room in this sector."

"I won't."

"Your response is not compatible with expectations of compliance."

"So?"

A panel slid open, and a rod extended from the torso of the discipline bot, pointing in her direction. A tiny crackle of blue light arched between two prongs on its tip.

"Reconsideration is suggested."

She gritted her teeth and pointed. "He pushed me into the airlock and tried to kiss me. Why should I be punished?"

The bot's antennae swung toward the open airlock door. There was a brief pause as it scanned the identification of the prone boy.

"Is Marcus injured?"

"I hope so."

"I have signaled a medical technician," the bot said. "You will accompany me to the Discipline Room." The bot swiveled back to her, but by then, she was ready. She opened her hand to reveal the ID badge she had removed from her uniform moments ago.

"Easy-peasy," she said, and she attached the badge's magnetized back to the airlock door before edging away.

☣

"You know," said the Registrar a short while later, "this continuing pattern of misbehavior makes it hard for me justify a request for your placement in the scholastic program," She ran a hand through her short, greying curls and regarded the young woman across the table.

The girl said nothing.

"I know what you're doing, so don't think you're fooling me," said the Registrar. "You get tired of Habitat Three-Four, so you act up, assault a boy in an airlock, and modify your badge, which takes a bit of skill, by the way, and then lead a D-bot on a chase. Then you're sent by the Controller to the Command module for a talking-to from me. Is that about right?"

The girl looked down at her hands.

"You've got another year until you transition from Habitat Three-Four to an ALW module."

"Yes, ma'am," said the girl, in a small, dismal voice.

"I want to see you in the higher scholastics. Your scans show you're bright, and we'll soon need three new engineers to replace the aging."

"Um," the girl began, but the Registrar silenced her with a glance.

"Maybe you would rather work in waste processing?" asked the Registrar. A shadow of a sneer flicked across her unmasked features, rendered them unattractive. "Or teach children in a habitat?"

"No, ma'am," said Sarah.

"I thought not," said the Registrar. "Bright minds need to keep busy. I've transitioned you early."

"Ma'am?"

"Don't get too excited, this isn't a reward for your behavior, and you won't go into scholastics until I say so."

"What will I do?"

"I've scheduled you for a orientation in remote reclamation. That should give you plenty of time alone to think about your future before you're permanently assigned."

"Yes, ma'am."

"That will be all." The Registrar turned away and scrolled through a workpad imbedded in the tabletop.

The girl stood up to leave. She hesitated at the white door.

"Sire," she began.

"Don't call me that," said the Registrar curtly, without a glance at her. "I'm not a sire any longer, not to you or anyone else."

☣

Transition was a rapid and cursory event. A human technician handed her a packet of new clothing and escorted her to the shuttle traveling to an Adult Living and Working module. Sarah learned that the major difference between the Habitat life of her adolescence and the ALW module was the color of the uniforms. As a child in the Nursery, she had worn blue; in Habitat Three-Four, orange; and now in Adult Living, her uniform was gray. It fit better than her tight orange one but pulled awkwardly under one arm. She still wore a bio-mask, as did most citizens of the orbital modules, to prevent rapid spread of common contagions that the air system failed to screen out.

The corridors were more crowded, and the food tasted the same. Her room was smaller, and she shared it with an older woman, Lindsey, who previously had the room to herself and did not appreciate the new arrival. Less talk passed between adults as they moved through the corridors, but at least there were port windows in the common areas, and no boys tweaked her breasts.

She started training the day after she arrived. Three older men and a middle-age woman, apparently unsuited for other adult tasks, were her fellow trainees. The reclamation trainer, a rotund woman with thinning yellow hair, showed the trainees images of reclaimer mechs on a viewscreen while the trainees ate stale boxed snacks. Then they ran stage one simulations. Each of the students took turns in a unit that looked like a chair with a series of electrodes lining the back.

"Sit back all the way, now," said the trainer when it was Sarah's turn. "Your head has to touch all the electrodes."

The electrodes felt cool and hard against her scalp on three sides. The trainer slid a head clamp into place. Her arms and legs were also clamped into position, not uncomfortably.

"Relax and just think about moving your legs."

"I can't."

"Close your eyes, dearheart," said one of the older men.

She closed her eyes and felt a jolt. There was a sound, like static on a disconnected monitor, and she saw Earth. With her eyes closed, she could see open space bathed in low, warm light. The vista seemed limitless, a flat floor that went on beyond the limits of her vision in the mech viewscreen.

"I'm frightened," she said.

"It's just like the vid," said the trainer's voice. "Think about moving your legs."

She ventured a glance in the direction of her should-have-been legs and saw the reddish surface far below the towering mech. With effort, she lifted one virtual leg and took a tentative step forward.

"Don't hold your breath," said the trainer.

Another step, and then another and another. Excitement thrilled through her. She walked and walked across the surface alone; no pressing bodies, no sound but her own rapid breathing, no walls. She looked up from the ground, and gasping, came to halt. The sky was lit in a burst of fire as the sun crested the horizon.

Awe gave way to vertigo, and the horizon swayed. A cracking noise, and she opened her eyes; five anxious faces looked into hers.

"It's all right, just breathe." The trainer removed the girl's mask and unclamped her head and arms.

"Grab that empty box over there," said the other woman. One of the three men, gruff but kind, placed the flimsy plastic food container in Sarah's hands.

She promptly vomited into the box.

After a few more weeks of simulations, she learned that she could ignore her body entirely, and the group began training on the mechs. There were drillers, loaders, haulers and sorters. She enjoyed working the haulers that crawled across the landscape, moving freely under the sky to the sorting depots where rubble was graded by robots for plastics, metals and calorie-rich material.

"Why don't they program robots to do this hauling?" asked another driver, scrawny and tall. They both stepped out of their upright chambers, rubbing tired eyes. His legs were too long for the standard gray uniform.

"I guess it's better this way," said Sarah. "I kind of like driving the remotes."

"Eh?"

"I said I like it," she said.

"Want to switch?"

The first shift assignments put Sarah on a loader and the tall man, Gerald, on a hauler, so they traded. She spent six days hauling loads to the central depot from other locations. She started every morning at sunrise, eastern hemisphere; a robot technician, which replaced the trainer, clamped her into a chamber. An auto-timer switched on, and she drove the hauler for four and one-half hours before it switched off again. Sometimes she'd do two shifts if another driver was out.

She sought the sky. The kaleidoscopic ceiling of the morning glowed in reds, oranges, blues and purples above the rutted tracks and excavation pits. The Controller chided the girl more than once as her attention, not to mention the hauler, drifted from scheduled tasks while she gazed upward.

"It's exhilarating," she said to her roommate, in one of their shared moments between shifts. After some initial awkwardness, the older woman had warmed to her presence. Lindsey worked as an environmental engineer, and though she seldom spoke of it, she took pride in what she did and looked down on her roommate's work.

"I don't see how." Lindsey continued shoveling something pink and noodle-like into her mouth from a box.

"Really, it's fun." Sarah leaned back against the bulkhead framing her bed, hands behind her head.

"Sounds like you need to experience actual fun, so you have a better basis for comparison," said Lindsey, laughing with her mouth full. "All you do is read mech files and talk about mechs."

"It's the sky. You should see it! Everything feels so open."

"But you aren't really there."

"Well, it feels like I am." Sarah smiled and then put on a pout. "Why do you have to take the fun out of it?"

"Because I know how to have some fun," said Lindsey, tossing her used box down the recycling chute. "Come to the rec suite with me, I'll teach you how to play jump-pong."

Spry for her age, Lindsey turned out to be very good at jump-pong. Sarah caught on quickly to the basic rules, but disliked dashing back and forth. When she jumped, her too-large breasts bounced painfully and made her feel self-conscious. She made a few feeble attempts to serve the little red ball and then sat on the sidelines when her roommate invited joiners for doubles. The rec suite quickly became crowded; she made her apologies to Lindsey and slipped out.

In the noisy common room, she passed a port window. She stopped and looked out over the planet below.

"Afrika," she said to no one in particular, and then more softly, "sector five." Her breath condensed in a mist on the window.

☣

"You're going to do it, aren't you?" she asked the older driller.

"Eh?" said Gerald.

"Is it true that you're going to stage two?"

"Who told you?" He stretched, and his long legs seemed stiff.

"Technician A-5," she said, tilting her head in the now-silent bot's direction.

He frowned, rubbing his forehead where the strap had rested. "Yes, I'm going, soon. A unit needs replacing."

"Do you think I could?"

"You're too young," he said, with a shake of his head. "Controller's not going to allow it. Maybe when you're old and useless like me." He waved a finger at the stage two unit in the corner.

"Can I watch, when you go?"

"I guess."

They sat together on the bench for a while, looking at the machine. An auto-timer chimed, and Tech A-5 whirred down the row to assist another driver.

"What do you want to do a thing like that for?" said Gerald, rubbing a rheumy eye. "Downloaded, stuck on the surface all the time. You'd miss your real body, after a while, young as you are. But not me."

"I wouldn't miss this body," she said, looking down at the white floor, and then at the window in the door that led to the crowded corridor.

"They don't live forever, you know."

"I know."

"Power outage or surge or a crash, and you're done, like the one I'm replacing. Unit memory got lost."

"I'd like it," she said. "It's quiet."

"It *is* that," he said with a little smile.

She had been running haulers and drillers for about eight months when she found the pit. She was on a driller in sector seven, and the ground collapsed beneath her. The mech slid facedown into the trench of soft earth, so deep she could see down in the dark crevice, but not far. The driller gave a groan that she felt rather than heard, and navigation displays went dark.

With a flick of thought, she switched on a headlight.

She saw shapes in the spotlight of her beam, round and white, straight and gray, piled deep and thick. The collapsed trench was over fifty feet wide and filled with human bones.

All around her in the pit, eye sockets seemed to gaze at her from empty skulls, some with leathered skin still stretched tight. She felt a thrill of horror, a sickness in her belly miles away, then unexpected joy. The bones of these dead lay in the earth, touching the soil of the planet in a way she never could. These dead had walked upon the earth with their feet, touched the ground with their hands, seen the sky with their own eyes. Unmediated, the people whose bones lay collected here by the thousands had lived on the planet of their birth with no virtual filter between them and the world.

A readout in her heads-up display flickered and the voice of the Controller said, "Please report status."

"I'm stuck." She mentally worked for a moment to move the mech, with no result.

"Another driller is being diverted to your unit's coordinates," said the Controller in soothing tones. "Your shift is concluded."

"No, wait!" Sarah cried. She heard the tell-tale crackle that signaled disconnect from the mech interface, and opened her eyes in the white chamber aboard the station.

A single tear shed for envy of the dead slid down and spattered on her gray uniform.

☣

She was reading a third manual on mechanical engineering when the notice came. She'd been assigned a week of recovery time after the pit collapse, and by happy circumstance, Lindsey had been called away to another module to repair a malfunctioning environmental system. To enhance her solitude, Sarah was enjoying another day of relative quiet, as the occupants of the noisy room next door were both ill and confined to quarters. A tiny *plink* alerted her to the arrival of the clear plastic notice as it dropped down a pneumatic tube into a slot bearing her number.

Sarah read the notice twice before its meaning registered. She had been given permanent assignment, but not in the scholastic program as the Registrar had suggested. Not to study and then be apprenticed in engineering, as she had hoped. The notice, generated by the Controller based on her intelligence and genetic profile as well as cold calculation, assigned her to Nursery Three as a Sire.

A breeder. For the next eight years, at least, she was expected to bear children for the expanding Habitats.

On the bottom of the rectangular slip, there was an addendum, a note from the Registrar. *You've got my hips*, it read.

"Balls," she said.

☣

Gerald's stage two upload, scheduled for the beginning of the morning shift, had been postponed because of technical problems with the suite technician bots.

Sarah met Gerald in the common room, and they stood looking out at sector five as it wheeled past over the edge of the horizon. They walked through the halls towards the reclamation suite, mindful of the jostling crowds of gray-suited adults making their way to the afternoon shift.

"You sure?"

Sarah nodded.

Gerald's face crinkled under the bio-mask as he gave her a smile.

They stopped at the door of the reclamation suite, and Gerald handed Sarah his ID badge.

"Sure it's gonna work?" he asked.

"Easy-peasy," she said. She pulled her bio-mask down to her chin and planted a kiss on Gerald's wrinkled cheek.

"If they ask me, I'll just say you stole it, okay?"

"Alright."

She turned and went into the suite. The door *snicked* shut behind her.

"Good afternoon, Gerald," said the technician bot. "Are you prepared for your stage two upload?"

"Yes," said Sarah, and she strapped into the uploader for the last time.

Elmer Bank

Emily Capettini

Elmer Bank had never taken a wife. He maintained that it was not for lack of available women—there were, after all, brothels to satiate a man's most primal need. It was because he lacked the time, busy as he was. The women with whom Elmer had flirted and attempted to take out to dinner would tell you differently. Sandwiched between clothes and a haircut twenty years out of date was a resourceful and industrious mind, but not one that made enough money to keep a contemporary woman comfortable.

Elmer was very much aware of his unpopularity as he walked down the street, glancing over at the young things striding by on heels that stretched thin their already scrawny legs. Mismatched, thought Elmer, adult shoes on a child's feet.

One turned and sneered at him, looping an arm through her friend's as they disappeared around a corner.

"Bank!"

Elmer turned away to see a handsome, lanky man striding his way.

"Douglas." Elmer had hoped he could sneak off before Douglas clocked out. He sighed and waited for Douglas to catch up.

"How are you, old man?"

Elmer was rewarded with a hearty clap on the back and a firm handshake. Patrick Douglas never skimped on enthusiasm, Elmer noted with some distaste as he covertly wiped his palm on his pant leg. And that was all well and good for those who didn't bruise easily.

"Not bad, thank you… and yourself?"

"Fantastic, just fantastic." Douglas slung an arm over Elmer's shoulders. "What do you say I treat you to a pint, and we discuss my day?"

"Well, I—"

"Splendid!"

And Elmer had no choice but to follow. He wasn't a fan of Douglas, who was always using words like "splendid" and "pint" and other sheer nonsense only understood in Europe. Douglas liked to talk about himself a great deal, yet he was always the one with women on his arms, no matter the setting—even at his own mother's funeral for Christ's sake.

"Never liked the old witch," Douglas had confided later. "Wouldn't let me have a puppy as a kid—what kind of mother doesn't let her only son have a puppy?"

"Did you hear about one of those South American countries?" Douglas interrupted Elmer's thoughts. "They actually made a *truce* with their women! A truce between them and us, can you imagine?" Douglas hooted, shaking Elmer.

"Well…" Elmer floundered. "They'll learn what we did, soon then, won't they."

Douglas laughed again. "That's what I like about you, Bank! Simple, straight shooter!"

Elmer said nothing and allowed himself to be dragged inside the bar. He could use that drink after all.

The women flocked to Douglas from the moment he set foot inside. It was a younger crowd this time of the day, and Elmer knew this was why Douglas wanted a drink. The women, just barely old enough for marriage, hardly glanced at Elmer. His smartly-parted hair glimmered in the dim lighting, and he was sneered at next to Douglas' kilowatt grin and three-piece Italian suit. The man positively reeked of money and the promise of luxurious living. While Elmer and Douglas didn't have the same income, Elmer preferred to tuck it away, a sturdy little amount in a sturdy little savings account. As a matter of fact, Douglas would be out of a job, if Elmer weren't around. Why, just this morning, Elmer had pulled Douglas out of a scrape because the idiot hadn't bothered to crunch the numbers he'd been assigned. Ruined the paper crane Elmer had been folding when Douglas stormed into his office. "Too busy looking for a missus," Douglas had claimed. "The boss ought to be proud of me, really, keeping those women in their rightful place! Sowing my wild oats and all that!"

"I'm not sure… does the boss… approve?" Elmer had tried.

Douglas gave him a withering look. "Just crunch the numbers for me, Bank."

Elmer sighed and returned to the instructions on screen. Some new kind of defense, he assumed, even though the war had been over for some time. There were still rumbles of insurgency in the women-friendly corners of the nation—knitting circles, book clubs, that sort of thing.

Elmer smoothed out the wrinkles where he had crunched the paper in surprise and delicately pulled. The paper crane sprung into shape.

"Origami?"

Elmer jumped. "Oh, hello, Emma."

"Didn't think you were much of an artist, Elmer." Emma was a small woman with dark hair twisted into a bun at the back of her neck, as was standard issue for all female workers. Emma had only been his secretary for around a year—since the war had come to a close—but she moved around the office with an easy grace that Elmer envied.

"It's nothing."

Emma had walked forward then and taken the paper crane. "Well, I think it's lovely." She toyed with it for a moment, refolding. Emma tugged on both ends, and its wings flapped obediently. "There." She set the crane down on the desk and placed a cup of coffee next to it. As she reached down to wipe up something, Elmer caught a glimpse of the elegant, tawny lines winding around her wrist and up her forearm, disappearing into her sleeve. It had indicated her rank, once.

"Um. Thank you."

"Of course, sir," Emma said with another tight smile. She walked back to her desk with the soft-footed movements of an assassin, the barcode tattooed on the back of her neck grinning at Elmer as she went.

"Bank! Those numbers!"

Elmer set the crane on top of his monitor and, with a smile, went back to work. He didn't even frown when Douglas barged back in and knocked aside the graceful creature, calling Elmer a useless sentimentalist.

"Bank!" Douglas yelled, snapping Elmer back to the present. "The ladies were just asking me… what *do* you do with all your money?"

Elmer looked into his drink and waited for the laughter to pass.

He didn't know what Douglas did with his income, but from what Elmer had seen of his wardrobe and his car, there was probably not much left by the end of the week. Confirmed bachelor was the popular term for it. Imbecile was likely more appropriate. Economical sense was not something Elmer could parade around, wearing it on the sleeve of his thrift-store suit. Women needed someone to support them; their wages were hardly anything to live on, something instituted to keep them more firmly in one place this time around.

Elmer left not long after, driven away by the hordes of women crushing in on Douglas. No wonder they had lost the war, Elmer thought with a grumble, silly things were blinded by a heavily-bleached smile. Mosquitoes to the bug zapper.

The street stretched in front of him, clusters of dimly-lit windows staring down at him. There were movements in the windows and several were open. It was almost the hour of business for this area of town. The sun was low in the sky.

"Lookin' for company, mister?" the girl called from her window, one pale shoulder peeking out from her leopard-print ensemble, a wolfish glimmer in her eyes.

Elmer shook his head and, with a hunch in his shoulders, scurried further down the street. He ducked through a dank alley, rushing past several other prostitutes. It was foolish of him, Elmer knew, refusing prostitutes when it was commonly accepted and normal to hire their services. There was something about it that unsettled him. The payment part, he supposed, or the barcodes, the way they'd all been categorized and stamped.

"Think of it as a dowry, if you're that uptight about the whole damned matter," Douglas had scolded once, when Elmer refused a girl who had approached. "Can't have love without money, old boy."

Head spinning, Elmer emerged onto a quieter street, better lit.

Half-priced reprints! proclaimed a smiling advertisement. *PAPER WIFE—REDUCE YOUR COST OF CLOTHES—EASY TO USE. PERFORATED, JUST PUNCH OUT AND ENJOY.*

A bright arrow beamed at Elmer, pointing to a small building with clean, simple lines. Elmer hesitated a moment. He had never been able to afford one when they were in demand…

The salesman that greeted him was far too eager, far too enthusiastic when gripping Elmer's hand. He was a short man with thinning hair.

"What can I help you with?"

"I, er… saw your advertisement?" Elmer felt utterly foolish.

The salesman revealed gums lined with yellowing teeth, a broken down amphitheater with no one left to mop up the grime. He directed Elmer to their extensive selection: Blonde, brunette, redhead, tall, short, curvy, thin—any and everything a man could ask for. Reasonably priced, too (*never pay for dinner again!* said the box).

"Are you looking for someone in particular?"

Elmer glanced over at the salesman, slouched near the almost full shelves of Bottle Blonde. He let his head roll to the side.

"Any… preferences?"

Elmer looked at him again. For a brief, uncomfortable moment, he could see the frayed edges of other people's fantasies sticking out from the cracks in the salesman's teeth, collected and ferreted away. Elmer turned back to the wall and blindly grabbed a box from the next shelf.

Raven-haired beauty, it read. *Aquamarine eyes, freckled, docile.*

The purchase was slipped into an opaque plastic bag and Elmer was wished, rather sarcastically, a good time. So, on that dreary evening, Elmer Bank went home and made himself a wife.

The instructions were flexible, encouraging Elmer to choose the shape best suited to his needs, as well as a hairstyle. *However,* read the instructions, *please be sure to do all editing before total assembly. G.B. Shaw, Inc. is not responsible for any damage done to you, your household, or the product.*

Here goes, thought Elmer, brandishing a pair of scissors.

He wasn't sure what he was looking for as he cut shape and length into the hair. The hard part would be twisting and shaping the tissue paper, fashioning a body type that would support itself and stand up in a slight draft. As Elmer clumsily sculpted the soft paper, he brushed off a growing anxiety. This might have been a very terrible idea.

He needed a drink.

The paper wife was waiting for him when he returned with a tumbler, propped up against the sofa and staring blankly in his direction. Elmer lingered in the doorway, giving it—or her, he supposed—a critical eye. He sipped at his drink. She remained motionless.

You complete idiot, Elmer scolded himself, what did you expect? A welcome?

With a firm *clink*, Elmer set his empty glass down on the nearest table. He crossed the room, aiming to throw out the packaging and ridiculous female *art craft* before any of his neighbors saw. As he bent to gather up the remains of the box, something swept close to his ear. Elmer yelped, dropping the box and whipping around.

The paper wife's head drooped to one side, staring at Elmer with factory-printed eyes. She retracted her arm, turning it bonelessly, and Elmer shuddered. She frowned, crinkling, and reached for him again.

"Stay—stay back!" Elmer snapped, panic bubbling in his stomach.

She swayed forward, feet shuffling, fluttering in a draft from the kitchen. Her arms flowed forward in some kind of gesture. Elmer glanced down and grabbed the owner's manual lying at his feet. He ducked behind the sofa and flipped it open.

Rule number one with your paper wife: do not panic. Remember, she is your wedded wife, and you must take excellent care of her.

Elmer skipped ahead.

Rule fifty-four: once your wife is awake, she will only be able to speak words that you have taught her. Simply press down the tab located on the back of her right shoulder to record.

Rule fifty-five: be sure your wife knows the connotations of the words. We at Shaw® do not, in any way, promote vulgar conversation in public.

In the back of the manual was a glossary of gestures and signs. Elmer peeked over the back of the couch.

Hello, his wife gestured, how are you, husband? The overhead light illuminated the freckles on her face.

Docile, Elmer told himself, she's docile, remember. Dociledociledociledocile. Get up. Slowly, now, no sudden movements;

don't want to frighten her. She might tear something, thought Elmer, swallowing a hysterical giggle.

She stared at him blankly, waiting.

"H… hello," Elmer said.

She crinkled again. Elmer wondered if the folds counted as dimples.

"I, um. I've never done this before." Elmer winced. "I mean! I've never paid—no! Well, I *haven't*, but that doesn't *mean*…"

The paper wife continued smiling, and Elmer swore he saw her hide a giggle behind one smooth hand. He clasped the back of his neck; this was not going to plan.

"What's your name?"

She tilted her head, frowning.

"You… haven't you got a name?"

She made another arm movement, pointing at the user manual.

Elmer opened it. *You are free to name your wife. We at Shaw® know the importance of a name and we encourage you to choose a believable name, suitable to the sort of woman you would bring home to your parents. The use of Internet name generators is acceptable, but discouraged.*

"Portia," Elmer blurted out. "How about Portia?" Then, Elmer reached forward and shakily pressed the tab along the back of her shoulder. "Portia," he said, slower.

"Portia," she repeated obediently.

Elmer let out a breath. Maybe this wouldn't be so bad. He reached for the tab again. "Hello."

"Hello!"

"How are you?"

"How are you!"

Elmer laughed, feeling his hysteria dissipate. His wife grinned at him, and there was an endearing toothy quality to her smile. Elmer found himself cautiously touching her elbow as he taught her phrases.

The front doorbell rang. Elmer froze, panic creeping up along his spine. He glanced wildly about the room, looking for something to hide Portia behind. Elmer flung back the dusty old Oriental rug on the floor.

"Quick!" he blurted, motioning.

The doorbell rang again.

Portia was silent and unmoving. Elmer seized her by her shoulders and swung her around. She looked startled when Elmer knocked her legs out from under her and tugged the rug over her head. Elmer ran to get the door and yanked it open.

"Mrs. Baker!"

"Oh, good, you are home, Elmer!" Mrs. Baker enthused, inviting herself in and shoving a pan of baked goods Elmer's way. "I saw your car in the driveway, and I had hoped I would get a chance to talk to you. Not very neighborly, the way you're always rushing inside without even a wave in my direction." She smiled at him and seemed about to pat his cheek. "Why, you'd think you had something to hide!"

Mrs. Baker smiled pleasantly at the stunned look on Elmer's face and bustled into the kitchen.

"Oh, don't mind me, dear. I won't ask what kinds of defense and weaponry you're cooking up at that government job of yours."

Elmer stared after her. He could hear her opening the refrigerator and rooting around inside. Soon, a steady stream of soft *thunks* drifted down the foyer to where Elmer was standing.

"You really ought to keep an eye on these things." Mrs. Baker called. "This milk is nearly a week old!"

"Mrs. Baker, you don't have to—"

"Of course I have to! Who else is going to take care of this? And no buts, you just make sure the vacuum's brought here so I can vacuum up what you've swept under the rugs."

Elmer bolted from the kitchen, frantically gathering up Portia and the paper wife packing materials. He then ran up to his bedroom and slammed a door behind him. Elmer leaned against the closed door for a long moment, trying to catch his breath. Mrs. Baker was a sweet, neighborly woman who had murdered her no-good husband.

Better find that vacuum for her.

Much calmer, Elmer came down the stairs and fetched what she asked for.

"Here you go, Mrs. Baker."

"Thank you, Elmer. Now don't mind me, you just go back to whatever you were doing." Mrs. Baker pointed at him with the nozzle of her cleaning spray. For a moment, Elmer could see her finger on a trigger, safety released.

Elmer felt the color drain from his face. He smiled weakly.

"Oh, my! Are you sure you're eating enough, dear? You look as though you may just drop where you're standing!"

"Yes, I'm... er, fine. Thank you."

Elmer fled. Again, he sprinted up the stairs and back into his bedroom. Elmer appreciated Mrs. Baker's good intentions, especially after his parents had passed away when he was hardly out of school, but sometimes... well, it was difficult to forget. Mrs. Baker was one of the women known for kicking off the inital fighting for War of the Sexes. Her husband was a gambling cheat and she, fed up with serving, cooking, cleaning, and hiding her precious little money in a tin can in the basement rafters, had calmly tottered downstairs, retrieved the silver pistol he had been given upon retirement, and disposed of the menace in her life. Reports had piled in after that: lying, cheating, abusive, manipulative—*no man was safe!*—and as things often do, the sudden outbreak of women *not taking it anymore* erupted into war.

A long, bloody war. Nearly ten years and the women had stopped at nothing—assassins, secret agents, spies, ambushes, and guerilla warfare were only the humble beginnings to their schemes. A miracle the men had won, really. "Just like ol' Lafayette and Washington scraping together a country!" Douglas had proclaimed on the day their victory was announced, spilling lager down Elmer's front. Elmer remembered being impressed; he often forgot that Douglas had had an excellent (and very expensive) education.

Portia crinkled from where Elmer had left her, crumpled on the floor. Elmer hurried over to unfold her, nervous apologies on his lips.

"Sorry. Didn't want rumors getting started. You wouldn't believe how things travel around here."

She made another motion.

Elmer scrambled over to the packaging debris, tearing through the pile until he found the manual again.

Would you like me to make you dinner, husband? she signed with a smile.

Elmer felt more of that hysterical laughter bubble up in his throat. "I shoved you away like a piece of trash and you want to make me dinner?" he paused. "How can you cook? Won't you incinerate?"

Portia motioned again with a glare, and Elmer paged through the manual.

"Hel*lo*," Portia snapped after a moment.

Elmer looked at her, startled. A giggle slipped out. "I suppose I ought to teach you more words."

Elmer spent the rest of his afternoon locked up in a room with his paper wife, teaching her phrase after phrase. Were anyone else looking in on them, Elmer would have thought himself insane. Buying a wife was normal enough now. Paper wives had been rare during the war, a marker of status for those rich enough to purchase them, but intended only to be replacements until the real women were brought under control.

Mrs. Baker left, as she always did once she was done cleaning cobwebs from the corners of Elmer's house, and by the time Elmer noticed life outside of the cozy room, the sky had darkened to a sleepy aubergine.

"We'll start again tomorrow?"

"Yes, husband."

Her voice was soothing with a plush undertone. Elmer swept out of the room to prepare for bed with a silly grin plastered on his face.

⚠

Portia did not sleep, Elmer realized later, she shut down. It was a practical issue, he supposed. He had a mental image of Douglas switching off his paper wife and stuffing her in the closet to have a night out with the chums.

Nevertheless, Elmer made sure Portia had a place to sleep every night. When he did a little research, he found that she was able to read, and shortly thereafter, he decided to fill her room with bookshelves.

"What are those?" she asked him.

"They're books," Elmer replied, as he wrestled a box into the room. "My mother's, mostly. She was the reader in the family." He rubbed at his nose. "They're, um—well, you can't really buy books like this anymore. These are ones my mother saved before they went electronic."

Portia tilted her head in a way that still gave Elmer a chill down his spine. Maybe he could talk her out of doing that.

"You want me to start reading, husband?"

"If you want to," Elmer told her, shelving. "You don't sleep, so I thought... maybe... and you're made of paper..." He trailed off, foolishly, and shrugged.

Portia was silent a long moment, and when she spoke again, it was without the affectation with which she had been packaged. "Thank you."

Embarrassed, Elmer had bidden her goodnight and retreated to his room.

⚠

The next morning, Emma entered his office with his morning coffee, hair loose around her shoulders.

"Good morning, sir," she greeted.

Elmer cleared his throat, looking up from some spreadsheet detailing explosives and their range. "Your hair—"

"Oh, do you like it? I just got it cut," Emma interrupted with a little smile. "And you're looking well today, sir."

"I am?" Elmer blinked.

"Happier," Emma clarified.

"Ah. Well."

She leaned against the doorjamb, sweeping her hair behind her shoulders.

It was a breach of strict protocol, Elmer reminded himself. All women were to wear their hair up, smoothed away from their identification numbers. It was a cautionary measure, meant to facilitate recognition scans.

"Found yourself a wife, have you?"

Elmer really should have said something to her, but instead: "I... er, what?"

"A wife," Emma said again, watching him carefully. "I overheard Mister Douglas going on about it. Says you must have found someone, the way you've holed yourself up in your house."

Elmer could feel the blush curling up from his neck. He should have anticipated Douglas would jump to such a conclusion—just because the man had four spare wives didn't mean... well, Elmer corrected himself, most other people did. Elmer just wasn't comfortable with the concept.

Marriage was an outdated practice, dissolved by the government just after the war. Sentimentality, they had said, had no place within a world power such as them. Marriage had been a woman's domain and anything with that marker would be removed from societal values. Now wife referred to any woman who was content to be persuaded and plied with gifts and money.

"I, uh. That is... no, Emma. No wife."

Emma's expression changed, just for a moment, but she had been Elmer's secretary long enough that he could recognize a shift in her mood.

"Would you mind running these files up to Douglas?"

"Certainly, sir."

Later, Elmer found a bright blue crane resting on his desk near a fresh cup of coffee.

❀

A week later, Portia came downstairs with a book weighing down her right side. She dropped it on the breakfast table and Elmer jumped at the noise. He peeked out from behind his newspaper, staring at the thick, leather-bound volume Portia had nearly thrown in his eggs.

"You want me to swallow..." and she motioned.

Elmer stared at her. "I beg your pardon?"

Portia made that motion again, the one that said, I don't know this word.

Elmer felt his face heat and dropped his eyes to the book, half-desperate. *The Complete Works of William Shakespeare*, read the worn-out spine.

Seeing his confused embarrassment, Portia flipped open the book to *The Tragedy of Julius Caesar*. "In here," she said, pointing.

Elmer frowned. Why would Portia—

Oh. He motioned Portia forward, depressed the tab on the back of her shoulder and said, very clearly, "Hot. Coals."

"Hot coals," Portia repeated. "You want me to swallow hot coals."

"No!"

"She has my name."

"But… no, no hot coals." How to explain this? "I just… gave you a name I liked. That I thought you might like."

Portia blinked. "You don't want me to imitate her," she said slowly, as if making a note to herself about it.

"No! Please."

Portia nodded.

"There's another one, you know." He reached for the book and turned to *The Merchant of Venice*. "This Portia is… well, she doesn't kill herself over a man. Maybe you'd like her."

Portia slipped her hand under the volume and lumbered away, presumably to read.

Elmer returned to his newspaper, resolving to take more care with names next time he had to give one to something that could talk back.

☣

Later that evening, Portia came up to Elmer again, this time without a book. She sat next to him on the sofa and waited patiently for him to finish the work he had brought home with him.

"Something wrong?" Elmer asked.

"I want to learn more."

Elmer sighed. "I know, but I have to finish this before tomorrow or the boss will have my head."

Portia pouted and slumped. She reached for a slim volume sitting on the coffee table and slowly flipped through it, her fingers slipping on the pages.

Elmer watched her. "Do you understand all those words?"

"Yes."

"I have an idea." Elmer got up from the couch and returned with a dusty roll of duct tape. Portia looked worried, but Elmer tried to give her an encouraging smile as he depressed the tab and taped it into place. Elmer returned to his seat next to Portia to finish up the work that Douglas hadn't bothered to do while Portia built her vocabulary quickly and efficiently.

Not bad for modern technology, Elmer marveled.

⚕

Not long after, Elmer went into work early. His office door was unlocked. He frowned; Elmer was sure he had locked it last night... or was that the night before? He shook his head and went in.

Well, at least there's nothing valuable in here, Elmer thought with a humorless smile. He set his briefcase down on the desk and was about to unbutton his coat when he spotted something silvery glinting in the low light.

An earring?

Sure enough, it was. Elmer picked it up and placed it on his desk.

"Oh, good morning, sir." Emma appeared in the doorway with a polite smile. "Is there anything I can get you?"

"Oh, ah, no, Emma," Elmer replied. He held up the earring. "I don't suppose this is yours?"

She jumped at the sight of it. "Oh! Where did you find it?"

"Just here, on the floor."

"Oh, I've been looking for it everywhere!" Emma blurted. She pocketed it with a hint of happiness in her usually bland smile. "Thank you."

Her hair was down again this morning, and Elmer found it easier to watch her return to her desk without a reminder of who she had been during the war.

⚕

A few mornings after the name incident, and after Portia had finished reading up on her more flattering namesake, Elmer was making himself some breakfast with Portia watching from a safe distance. The cooking question had never been resolved and Elmer thought it safer to keep her away from open flames. Portia had protested, but when Elmer insisted, she backed down obediently.

The doorbell screeched, piercing their peaceful morning. Elmer glanced over at Portia. He made a motion for her to sit, even as she rose to answer the door.

How odd, this playing hostess. Probably due to that Emily Post nonsense she's programmed with, Elmer recalled from the manual.

The doorbell rang again.

"Bank, open up! I know you're there!"

Elmer stopped short, staring at the front door in horror. Douglas? What on earth was he doing here?

"Bank! Come, come, I haven't all day!"

Elmer unlocked the door and opened it just a crack, peering through the opening. "Good morning, Douglas," he said with a poorly-concealed frown. "What can I help you with?"

"You can let me in for starters! It's bloody freezing out here, I'll have you know."

"I don't really—"

But Douglas, taller and broader than Elmer, pushed his way in, shaking unseasonable snow from his overcoat. He raked a glance over Elmer with a bit of a sneer on his face. "You aren't going in that, are you?"

Elmer glanced down at his clothes, meant for doing work around the house. He blinked. "Going where?"

"To the club! To find you a proper date for this business dinner in a few weeks."

Ah, Douglas had said something about that as Elmer was leaving work last week, he remembered now. Elmer didn't think he agreed to such a venture, but that was irrelevant. Protesting was pointless. It was worse than arguing with a stone statue; stone statues didn't spit.

"Husband?" Portia's voice slipped from the kitchen.

"What's this now? 'Husband,' eh?" Douglas slapped Elmer on the back in a distinctly "attaboy" manner. "Never thought you one for a bit of vice, old boy!"

"It's not… what you think." Elmer protested lamely.

"Oh ho ho, of course it isn't." And then Douglas *winked*.

Elmer was in trouble.

"I'll just go in and… greet the missus, shall I?" Douglas swept past Elmer, down the short hall to the warm kitchen.

Elmer ran after him, knowing it was useless to try and stop Douglas, but at the very least, he could implement some kind of damage control. He briefly entertained the idea of hitting Douglas over the head with a frying pan once he was in the kitchen and claiming that Portia and everything else was just some insane fantasy. Perhaps Portia had some kind of defense mechanism programmed into her, though likely not. Docile, Elmer reminded himself. Probably just blinks her doe-eyes and that's the end of it.

"Oh! Well, hello there, young lady!"

"Hello," Portia replied with a doubtful expression.

Elmer watched surprise flicker across Douglas' face. Then he grinned. "Ah, one of those classic paper wives, eh, Bank?"

Elmer said nothing and watched Portia.

"So then. What's your name, dollface?"

"Portia."

"Portia," Douglas repeated skeptically with a scowl in Elmer's direction. "Sounds like your choice of a name, Elmer. What's that, your friend Shakespeare again?"

"Would you like something to eat or drink?" Portia interrupted.

Douglas turned a charming smile on her. "Do you take rain checks?"

Portia glanced over at Elmer, fluttering in confusion.

"She doesn't know that word," Elmer told Douglas shortly.

"She doesn't know 'rain check'? What else doesn't she know?"

"Whatever I haven't had a chance to teach her yet."

A new smile crept onto Douglas' face, one that made Elmer flush in anger. "You get to *teach* her words? Why, that's the greatest thing I've heard yet!"

An overpowering sense of dread settled over Elmer. He wracked his brain—there *must* be some way to get Douglas to leave.

"… Bank! Bank, are you even listening?"

"I'm sorry, what did you say?"

"I asked what you'd already taught her." Douglas slapped Elmer's shoulder and shook him. "I have faith in you. Now! Tell me, 'husband.'"

Oh God, that wink again.

"Douglas, I don't really have the time," Elmer snapped, feeling stretched thin and overstressed. Weren't the paper wives meant to alleviate that, to have a relationship without the stress? "Do you have a reason for being here, or are you just lingering?"

Douglas stared at Elmer. "I beg your pardon?"

"I said—"

"Oh, I bloody well heard what you said! I've come to do you a favor, to keep you from moping over that silly little brunette secretary of yours—don't look so shocked, you really have no sense of discretion, and are you *mad*, man? You know she was a top assassin during wartime!—and this is the way you treat me? Your *only* friend?"

Elmer flushed, and a jumble of thoughts tumbled through his brain. Perhaps it was unfair to snap at Douglas—but he was just so overbearing—and Portia—Elmer sighed. He would give Douglas the benefit of the doubt over his good intentions.

"No need for the temper flare. I won't steal your new toy."

"Yes, of course," Elmer replied. "I suppose I'll go get ready."

Elmer went up the stairs to find something suitable to wear, digging through his sparse closet. Near the back, tucked under a pair of old sneakers, he found a blue gift box. Elmer vaguely recalled this being given to him at some office party a few years ago; clothing, he remembered. Elmer pulled out the box and opened it.

It's about time you started dressing up for the country club! My treat, old man. Wear it with confidence.

Of course it was Douglas who had given it to him, Elmer thought with a sigh. Reluctantly, he dressed and returned downstairs.

"Come on, dollface. It'll be fun," Douglas' voice drifted out from the kitchen.

"No thank you," Portia insisted, and Elmer could hear her feet *shifff* against the tile floor.

"You want to please your man, don't you?"

"That is not your business."

"Believe me, sweetheart, it is my business. Why, before I came along, the old boy was a Prufrock!"

Elmer peeked around the corner. Portia was giving Douglas an appraising look, but a glare lurked in the shaded corners of her eyes.

"You know… *in the room, the women come and go—*"

"*Talking of Michelangelo*, yes, I've read it," Portia snapped.

Douglas was clearly even more taken aback than Elmer. "*Read* it? How can you have *read* it? Someone *painted on* your eyes!" He floundered for a moment before sputtering, "Or even understood it! A book, the marker of all men's brilliance! You haven't even got a *brain* up there!"

Portia pointed at herself and said, quite firmly, "Paper."

Douglas gaped. "You mean to tell me there's some kind of psychic link between *species of paper*? That you and some book have a connection and *understand* each other?"

Portia's frown creased deeper, and her hand crumpled into a fist at her side.

Elmer decided it was a good time to interrupt. He strolled into the kitchen, shooting a suspicious look at Douglas. "Lively conversation you two are having."

"Er… yes, well, the old girl has some spark in her!"

Elmer glanced at Portia. She smiled warmly.

"I should hope not," Elmer replied with a smile in return. "She's made of paper."

Portia giggled and shuffled away.

Douglas was giving him that look again, a look that seemed to say, whatever has gotten into you, I don't like it.

"Well, then. Are we ready?"

Douglas turned and silently strode for the door. Elmer followed. He made no attempt at conversation, and they rode in silence until they reached the club.

"She's a bit too sassy if you ask me," Douglas said, finally. "A woman you paid for should know her *place*."

Elmer shrugged, allowing himself a private smile. He glided in after Douglas, humming happily as they took the scenic route. Douglas paused to greet and charm every well-dressed person they ran into. Sometimes he introduced Elmer, though on occasion, Elmer introduced himself. It made the vein in Douglas' forehead stick out, Elmer observed with giddy amusement.

They emerged into a lounge area, where several of Douglas' cohorts were slumped about. Old cigars and empty brandy glasses peppered every flat surface, and smoke hung lazily along the high-vaulted ceiling. After various greetings and several disdainful glances in Elmer's direction, Douglas held up his arms for their attention.

"Gentlemen, I have some news!" he clapped Elmer's shoulder with a grin that made Elmer nervous. "Old Bank here has bought himself one of those paper wives."

"Ah, splendid!" said one.

Another grinned, raising his glass. "Bet you're having fun."

"Ran through three of those, I did! Number four's made of stronger stuff, it seems!"

"Gentlemen, gentlemen, you haven't hear the *best* part yet." Douglas paused. "She *reads*."

"You don't say!"

"Why, how *quaint*."

"Well, you've got to do *something*. The blasted things aren't exactly built to withstand what they're *meant for*."

This was a terrible, terrible idea, Elmer thought. How on earth did he get talked into this?

"Did you say you're on your fourth, Thomas?" Douglas interrupted.

"Oh, yes. They don't cost much and I just set up the new one in front of 'James Bondage' while I'm at work, and by the time I get home, she knows all the words needed."

"Well, there you are, Bank!" Douglas grinned. "No need to have her read all sorts of outdated nonsense."

"Ah, and if you'd like her to *last*—"

"I don't think—" Elmer cut in.

"Oh come on, old boy, it's just some friendly advice."

Elmer opened his mouth to argue otherwise (he was severely doubting any "good intentions" now), but his protest was lost.

"Like I said, if you want her to last, you have to make sure you use protection!" The rest of the men around Thomas murmured in agreement. "Oh, and Elmer, you have to be gentle with her, remember. She isn't like a normal woman; she won't heal. Something I've learned the hard way, I'm afraid!"

"Oh, ho ho ho! There you go, old boy! It'll be time that you invested in some glue!"

Elmer, unfortunately, wasn't quick enough on his feet to be anything other than a part of the crowd. His exit was hardly graceful, but an exit was an exit, and Elmer would take a dumb, stuttering one over remaining in that room any longer.

He took a long walk home, the rapidly-cooling afternoon air calming him. As the walk cleared his head, however, Elmer began to mull over what Douglas and his cohorts had said. Perhaps this wasn't as smart of an investment as he had originally thought—a little company, that's all he had wanted. Portia was a piece of paper that was walking, talking, and perhaps not breathing, but she was intelligent enough to realize that herself. *Paper!* Flimsy paper! And unless he laminated her…

This was a problem. More than a problem. A *catastrophe*.

Elmer paused by a park bench and, after a moment, sat. There were children playing across from him in the park, kicking a soccer ball back and forth, while a dog ran between them. Elmer tipped his head, watching. He had wanted children when he was younger, but there had been too little time, too much career, and a war with which to contend. And now Portia…

Elmer saw a paper child enter the game, a happy, painted-on smile stretching wide across her face. The other children welcomed her, and she nudged the ball around the circle.

Elmer smiled. Perhaps he was being too pessimistic. Maybe it could work out. Paper wives were catching on, now that they were affordable. Portia wouldn't be anything new to the neighborhood. Why, she was positively charming. Everyone would adore her and—

The neighbor's dog had reentered the circle. It barked and bounded for the paper girl. She shrieked happily, playing. The other kids ran over. One yelled for his mother. The little girl's shrieks grew louder, panicked, and the sounds of ripping paper tore through the beautiful day. A man dashed towards them, presumably the father, and pulled the dog away. The dog yapped playfully, wet scraps of paper stuck to its muzzle. Half of the little girl's face drifted around Elmer's feet with wide, blank eyes and a frown torn in two. The face was crumpled and curled in on itself, a jagged rip where her nose should have been.

"Sorry," said one of the kids as he grabbed the scraps of paper. "Didn't mean to litter."

Elmer watched, something twisting in his stomach, as the children laughingly chased scraps of their little friend around the park and then shoved her remains into the nearby recycling bin.

Recycle, reuse, said the bin and it had pictures: newspapers, tin cans, glass bottles and... an outline of a female form.

Elmer felt the bottom drop out of his stomach. He scrambled up from the bench, hurrying home. Elmer raced up the steps and slammed the front door behind him.

"Portia?" he called shakily.

"In the kitchen, husband."

Elmer tossed his coat to the side and found Portia. She smiled at him from behind the counter and next to her...

"Emma? What on earth—"

"I brought the files you asked for. But you weren't home and Portia and I started talking..."

"I'm making you dinner!" Portia said brightly. Something chirped and Portia turned. "Oh, there it is."

"I—dinner?"

Emma had hurried around to the oven as Portia stepped back. Emma wrapped a dishtowel around her hand and pulled out the casserole. Elmer blinked at the pair of them, watching as Portia cleared the bowls into the sink, and Emma went to wash them. Surely he must be imagining this scene.

"Why so shocked, husband?"

"Well... nothing, I guess," Elmer answered. There was something peculiar here, he felt, but there was no evidence that he should be as suspicious as he was. Odd.

"I invited Emma to stay for dinner."

"Oh. Wonderful."

"Is that all right, sir?"

"Yes, yes, of course," he fidgeted. "and, er... I suppose you ought to be calling me Elmer."

Emma beamed and turned to carry the heavier things to the table. As Portia set out the silverware, glasses, and plates, Emma turned off the oven and the burners. Elmer watched them work around each other in the kitchen, smiling as Emma smoothly avoided hitting Portia when she stumbled into Emma's path.

Perhaps the world was on to something with this spare-wives thing, Elmer thought. Having Emma around might mean children after all... but no, this was only dinner.

But wait. It was *dinner*. Didn't that usually bode well when a woman cooked for you?

"I hope you're not thinking about work, Elmer," Emma said shyly as she placed a tumbler of brandy in front of him. "It's important to relax during mealtimes."

"She's right," Portia agreed. "Wouldn't do for you to not be hungry for all this food we've made you."

"Oh, you didn't have to," Elmer began, though pleased. His face must have shown it, for both women smiled at him and took their seats at the table in the dining room, which had previously been covered in all kinds of graphs and charts—more work that Douglas had dumped on Elmer.

The food was exquisite, and Elmer took seconds, gulping his brandy.

"This is *delicious*," he announced, feeling warm and content. "And the brandy! Where did you girls dig it up?"

"Special recipe," Emma winked. "Would you like some dessert?"

Elmer, feeling bold, leant over the table and replied with a bit of a leer, "Maybe I ought to give you a hand in the kitchen."

A strange expression crossed over Emma's face, but before Elmer could consider it, she had tossed her hair and laughed, almost haughtily. She retreated to the kitchen, and Elmer watched the movement of her hips. He made to get up from the table—

"That's odd," Elmer commented. But, it wasn't commented, so much as… slurred. The ground swam under his feet. He grabbed for the edge of the table, and it slipped in his sweaty grip. "Portia," he started. "I. Something's wrong."

"That'll be the special recipe, husband."

"Emma?" Elmer strained to stay upright as the sound of her heels approached.

"I am sorry to do this to you, Elmer." Emma sighed. "You were one of the more tolerable ones, didn't even take advantage of the mistress clause in my secretarial contract."

"Or your poor, helpless wife," Portia added, coming to stand next to Emma.

"You two—together?" Elmer squeaked.

"Not initially," Emma told him. "I had originally planned on staging a fire, but then I properly met her. Not quite the model I saw during the war."

"You shouldn't have let me read all those books. Why name an obedient paper wife after a woman who uses wit and cleverness to take the power she deserves?" Portia tilted her head. "Didn't Douglas tell you how we learned women are dangerous?"

"You even let her see your research and calculations, leaving them carelessly about for anyone to take. Awfully nice of you to let us see the prototype weapons before they can be used against us."

Elmer's knees shook and ached. "How… Portia, how… I thought

you…" His legs gave out, and Elmer sank to his knees. His thoughts splashed and blended together. Portia, a woman who infiltrated a man's world and turned the tables in her favor.

Portia, Elmer's head spun as he stared up at his paper wife. Should have gone with the hot coals bit after all, he thought.

"*I never did repent for doing good, nor shall not now.*" Portia smiled fondly. "Goodbye, husband, thank you for the books."

"We won't kill you," Emma soothed. "And Douglas won't even blink when you tell him two guerilla fighters got the better of you."

"We do like you, you know," Portia added.

"In another time, things may have worked out." Emma bent, and her lips swept against his cheek. "War has never been a good time for happy endings."

Elmer scrambled for something, *anything*. "But… you won't be able to read them—the charts—they're in code—"

Portia's hand stuck to his sweaty cheek. Elmer focused on her face, fighting for consciousness. Her mouth curled and she said one word before Elmer lost the battle—and possibly, the war:

"*Paper.*"

Mouth

M. Svairini

She had a name, but tonight she would just be Mouth.

How delicious and perverse it felt to be addressed just by her gender, her primary genital area. Only a mouth. And the outfit that Will had sent her wear emphasized that status. Mouth salivated as she stepped into the red latex bodysuit. Her feet slid into the six-inch stilettos that protruded from the suit's two lower limbs. She pulled the sticky material up her plentiful body, stretching it tightly over the rolls around her hips and waist. Her fingers wiggled into gloves, and built-in kneepads let her know the position she'd be expected to take for the evening, if she was lucky. The jumpsuit was so tight that it was nearly translucent in places. The only opening was a hole in the hood, framing her dark, round face.

She painted on her bright red lipstain, shuddering as the moist aphrodisiac gel touched the six sensitive neuro-crystals in her lips. They sparked and sparkled. Almost of its own will, her tongue responded by shifting against the insides of her teeth. She heard herself panting lightly as she licked the sweet t-spot on the roof of her mouth. Perhaps she should masturbate to orgasm, just to take the edge off so that she could manage the hourlong ride on the Tube to Will's place in peace?

But then she looked at the clock: 7:45. The station was only minutes away, but in stilettos, she should give herself the extra time. And the outfit had one more piece: a mysterious triangle of red silk, with small metallic hoops attached to two of its corners. Earrings. She placed the one ring in each earlobe so that the veil fell just below her nose and across her mouth. The silk brushed against her lips so lightly that she felt naked. She would have to be careful of the wind that sometimes picked up when the trains came. She imagined a breeze lifting the veil, exposing her genitalia to everyone... Stop it, she told herself firmly. But she was already wet, and she swallowed hard.

☣

Mouth was old enough, just barely, to remember when people had lived up on the surface, before the Emergency. Children now grew up fearing the surface Tubes, and most of the younger generation preferred the slick new tunnelpods that allowed riders to avoid the view of Up There. There was even a movement to shut the Tubes down, with activists claiming they were riddled with air leaks that the government was covering up. Mouth didn't get involved in politics—her day job working for the Executive didn't allow it, for one thing—but she hoped the Tubes would stay open. She had always loved the red swirling air and fog, the ghosts and dragons you could imagine you saw out there, how it looked as if you could swallow and lick at the constantly shifting shapes, and they would taste of strawberries, blood, sex. She was already gazing out the thick plexi as she stepped onto the train, so at first she didn't realize people were staring at her.

The other riders looked away quickly, of course, and technically her dress was impeccable. Her sex was covered, which was the important thing. Others wore far less than her: Across the aisle a girl sporting a loincloth was nearly kickboxing in her seat, absorbed in a personal portable holo-game, while further ahead, two people wearing only aprons over their rear parts were alternating between whispers and outbreaks of giggling. But the fabric they wore was standard issue, thick enough to conceal their respective genitals... not sensual and flimsy like the bit of red silk that barely covered her own hole.

And besides, they weren't mouths, as 75% percent of legal prostitutes and 99% of illegal prostitutes were, according to the report Mouth had copy-edited that morning for the Executive. Of the four genders, mouths were the most likely to be arrested for crimes of perversity and solicitation; the most likely to drop out of school; yet ironically (she had nearly laughed aloud reading this line) the most likely to report "high" or "extremely high" levels of Life Satisfaction. Translation: Mouths do it better.

But respectable mouths avoided the taint of perversity, wearing gender-neutral colors and outfits that covered all of their parts. At work she dressed like everyone else: loose-fitting dress or pantsuit, headscarf wrapped just below her nose. In that quasi-uniform, no one was supposed to know if you were cock, pussy, ass, or mouth; all four genders were equal in the eyes of the law.

Somehow, though, everyone always knew. And Mouth could understand why restaurants had developed separate eating areas for mouths, even why coworkers excluded her from friendly lunches. If a mouth ate in public, it was awkward for everyone, easily crossing the line into blatant exhibitionism. Soon after her own Sorting, Mouth herself, used to going out with friends for ice cream, had found herself writhing in pleasure publicly as Chocolate Chip Creme de Menthe overwhelmed her newly Enhanced organ.

The Enhancements, ironically, were supposed to create equality. A century ago, around the same time the toxins on the Surface had banished people underground and all reproduction to the laboratory, neuro-sexologists had discovered a way to reroute all of the body's pleasure nerve endings to a primary area of choice or inclination. At puberty, you could choose, based on preference or a demonstrated inclination, whether you wanted to have your strongest pleasure center be your cock, cunt, ass, or mouth. Within a couple of generations, there were four genders instead of two, so patriarchal pronouns were phased out; everyone was now a *she*. Still, perhaps the human tendency toward hierarchy could not be averted altogether...

An older woman brought Mouth back to the present by plunking awkwardly down in the seat next to her. She wore just a knee-length pleated purple skirt, and Mouth was fascinated by her pale wrinkled teats hanging low on her torso, overlapping the waistband of the skirt by two or three inches. The woman noticed Mouth's gaze, and her eyes ran up and down Mouth's body in return, taking in the latex, high heels, kneepads, and finally resting on the delicate red veil. "Headed for an exciting Friday night, are we, dearie?" she leered.

Mouth nodded politely before looking away. After a moment, the woman put her hand on Mouth's thigh and began to grope her, and Mouth did not stop her. Why should she? It felt good, and Will had given no orders regarding her activities before the party. After a few moments, the woman took Mouth's hand and placed it on her own crotch, where Mouth felt a bulge that had not been there when the woman sat down. So, she was a cock, then. Mouth pulled back her hand, wanting to keep it legal; touching someone's primary genitalia in public was a crime.

The woman paused, perhaps uncertain if her fondling was still wanted, so Mouth parted her legs and inched forward slightly as encouragement, and soon she felt fingers stroking her tightly outlined labia. These were usually no more sensitive than her toes or fingers, ever since her own Enhancements in puberty had rerouted all of her pleasure-nerve endings to her oral cavity.

But now, anticipation had sensitized all of her skin, so the fingers felt enjoyable. No one could see Mouth's tongue flicking at the perfect spot on her palate. Amid all the vibrations and sounds of the Tube, only the woman touching her felt the shudder that briefly overtook Mouth's whole body.

Out the window, the fierce filthy air shaped itself into teeth, lips, bodies merging and parting like flames.

☣

"Come in, my dear, we're just about to get started," Will said, kissing her lightly over her lips, and grinning as the surprise contact through the thin material made Mouth gasp. Will looked at her closely, taking in her flushed cheeks and glassy eyes, after-effects of her orgasm on the Tube. "But it looks like you've already gotten a head start, am I right?"

Mouth nodded, and Will made her describe the whole episode in detail as they walked downstairs to join the others. "And you didn't say a word to her, not even to say thank you?"

"She got off the train right afterward," Mouth said defensively.

"What a nasty little girl you are," Will said, just as they entered the party room.

A tall person Mouth did not recognize, with electric blue dreadlocks and a very young face, piped up, "And that's why you've brought them all here for me, isn't it, darling?" The stranger walked over to them and engaged Will in a deep, tongue-thrusting kiss that turned the temperature up in the room several degrees. Then she stepped back to examine Mouth. Her eyes raked over every curve, lingering at last on Mouth's veiled genitals, and Mouth felt self-conscious, objectified, and desperately hoping the girl-woman was pleased with her.

"Yummy," the woman said, licking her bare pink lips. Mouth felt like a piece of chocolate cake about to be devoured. "Shall we get on with it then?" others began to gather, and Mouth took the opportunity to study the scene.

Will was a cock, and her prominent position in the judiciary entitled her to more credits and larger living quarters than anyone else Mouth knew: a split-level apartment that took up three whole floors of a housing shaft. The unit's middle floor was the best place for a social event of this sort, since any sound would be buffered from the neighbors. Internal walls had been demolished, creating a large room that managed to seem sparsely furnished despite a king-sized bed in one corner, a baroque plum-and-gold sofa set, various fetish equipment and bondage devices, and an artificial fireplace around which the guests clustered. Mouth saw that the other two guests were dressed almost like her: latex jumpsuits color-coded by gender with built-in stilettos, kneepads, and convenient holes. It was obvious what their names were, at least for tonight: Ass, with a pretty orange scarf covering her rear, and Cunt, wearing a diaphanous purple thong that was already soaked. Cunt must have had an eventful trip here, too, though she didn't look quite as satisfied as Mouth was feeling.

Will and the unknown woman made up the rest of the group. Their outfits were black, made of a flowing chiffon-like material, beautifully tailored and flattering. Will wore a longish tunic over pants, the stranger a dress that fell below her knees and displayed her impressive cleavage. They would not have been out of place at an office party or evening function. In short, they were not dressed like whores, with their genders on display; they were clearly the mistresses of the evening.

"Time for the icebreaker, isn't it, darling?" the stranger said to Will, who smiled indulgently.

"Almost, my dear," Will said. "First let me do the introductions. In case anyone's blood is already flowing far from her brain, I'll state the obvious: Cunt, Ass, Mouth." Will gestured at each of them in turn, grandstanding as if hosting a much larger gathering, and then put her arm around the unknown woman's waist. "And this lovely creature is Aurora Arizmendi Azur. That's Mistress Azur, or just Mistress, to you lot. You can call me Mistress Will, or just Mistress, too. Your safeword for the evening is 'architecture,' although I doubt you'll need it; Mistress Azur prefers to manipulate you with pleasure, rather than pain, which I hope will not disappoint any of you too much. Now, Mouth, go into the bar refrigerator and bring out the bucket of ice. You two: Strip."

Mouth was conscious of rustling behind her as everyone followed orders. She was slightly jealous; was Will going to make her to serve the drinks while everyone else got to play? The ice cubes were fashionably shaped into cylinders about an inch in diameter and four inches long, making a lovely display in the silver bucket, which was engraved like a Grecian urn with scenes of couples copulating. When she returned, she was surprised to see that the others had removed only the flimsy fabric over their genitals, keeping the jumpsuits on. Will took the ice bucket from her and said, "You, too."

Grateful to be included, Mouth quickly undid her earrings and removed the veil. At once she felt more naked than if she were completely nude, with her painted, crystalline genitals throbbing and on display for everyone to see. She realized the others must be feeling the same way as she looked around, admiring them.

Cunt had three sets of visible labia, each unfolding out from each other like the petals of a rare flower, in various shades of pink and purple that seemed only slightly color-Enhanced. Her clitoris, however, was bright magenta, at least a centimeter in diameter, and perfectly round as a button, with a large neuro-crystal pulsing in the very center. It had no hood. Smaller crystals were sprinkled plentifully throughout the folds, in a v-shaped pattern that seemed to waver and wink at the room. Her entire vulva glistened with moisture, which dribbled out from the innermost folds in uneven rivulets escaping down her inner thighs. Mouth felt her salivary-erecto glands shift into overdrive as she contemplated licking up those tiny streams, following them to their source deep within.

Then Will made a sort of swirling-fingertip gesture toward Ass, to whom it was obviously a familiar cue; she immediately turned around and touched her toes, displaying large, creamy buttocks that parted to show an iridescent hole. Her ball sack and small penis, hanging down from the front, were also visible, though tightly encased in her orange latex outfit. An ass's Enhancements were mostly internal, and Mouth wondered what qualities had gotten Ass invited to this exclusive soiree. Taste? Capacity? Some sort of special neuro-sensations for one who penetrated deep inside?

"Part your lips, Mouth," Will said, which was easy to do, as she was almost panting already. "You aren't allowed to let your lips touch each other for any reason this evening. Like the other two, your fuckhole is to be open to us at all times. Is that clear?"

Mouth nodded. "Answer out loud," Mistress Azur commanded.

"Yes, thank you," Mouth said, pausing before continuing, "istress," which made everybody laugh.

"Oh, this is going to be very amusing!" Mistress Azur said, clapping her hands like a child. "Let's make her say lots and lots of sentences! Say 'My Mistress makes my mouth water.'"

"eye istress akes eye outh otter," Mouth said, somewhat miserably, drawing another peal of childish laughter from Mistress Azur and an amused, sadistic grin from Will; Mistress Will, she corrected herself in her mind. It would not do to make that mistake out loud.

"Icebreaker, icebreaker," chanted Mistress Azur impatiently. How old was she, anyway? It was impossible to tell, though Mouth knew Will, who was in her fifties, preferred mature women. At thirty-three, Mouth was one of the youngest women in Will's circle. The others seemed to be at least in their forties, as far as Mouth could tell.

Will addressed the three submissives, "As a sort of icebreaker game—well, it'll be more of an ice melter, I think—you will put on a show for us. We had thought we'd have you draw straws, but I think there's an easier way to decide who goes first. Don't you, my dear?"

Mistress Azur cocked her head quizzically.

"One of our guests has already had an orgasm this evening," Will explained. "So I think she should service everyone first, before she gets another one."

"It's only fair," Mistress Azur agreed. Mouth groaned inwardly.

"And Cunt looks more than ready for hers, don't you think, my dear?"

"But perhaps we should make her wait longer?"

Cunt, who had been looking hopeful, pressed her lips together. This reminded Mouth to keep her own mouth open, and as she listened to the Mistresses banter about the fate of their poor submissives, she licked her lips unconsciously.

Mistress Azur caught the gesture. "Our little Mouth is quite impatient, isn't she?"

"On your knees," Will said, and snapped her fingers, pointing to a spot on the floor facing her. Mouth crawled to the center of the circle, knelt in front of the Mistresses with her hands upturned on her thighs, and breathed deeply, enjoying the relief that this position always gave her: From now on, nothing would be up to her.

Finally, they decided that since Mouth had already come, and Cunt was exhibiting over-eagerness and generally whorish behavior, obedient Ass would get the first turn. The game was this:

Mouth would take a rod of ice between her lips. This itself would be excruciating, since her sensitive genitals were already swollen and overheated. She would use the ice-dildo, as well as her own lips and tongue, to service each of her co-submissives in turn. If the woman came close to orgasm, she could beg the Mistresses for release, and they would decide if she deserved it. If she failed to climax before the ice-rod melted, she was out of luck, and Mouth would be ordered to move on to someone else.

Mouth, whose genitals would be receiving more stimulation than anyone else during this game, was not allowed to come. She would only be allowed to beg for permission after everyone else in the room—including the two Mistresses—had had an orgasm. Therefore, it was in her best interests to bring everyone to climax as rapidly as possible.

☣

Ass was told to get on all fours for the game, while the Mistresses settled into a wide loveseat with Cunt between them. They strummed Cunt's labia casually, making them flutter open and closed. Cunt was already letting out small moans as Mouth knelt on the floor behind Ass. The bucket of ice was next to Mouth, and she bent over and picked up one of the rods in her mouth. It slipped, Mistress Azur tsk-tsked, and Mouth tried again, using her teeth this time to hold it steady.

The ice shocked every nerve ending in her tongue, lips, and palate. Her t-spot fired with pain as the frozen rod brushed against her palate. Mouth wanted to push it out of her orifice and into Ass's hole as quickly as possible.

But Ass was tight, and to relax the sphincter, Mouth had to take the ice deeper in her throat and then work the asshole with her tongue. As her hot mouth shrank the ice, she swallowed and managed to work her tongue an inch or so into Ass's hole.

Ass moaned with pleasure and pushed back toward her to get deeper penetration. Mouth braced herself, then reorganized her tongue to push the rod inside Ass's warm, dark orifice. The Mistresses cheered encouragement, which Mouth heard in a rather muffled way over the sound of her own slurping. Suddenly the frozen rod slipped out of her grasp, as Ass's hole suctioned it deeper. Mouth let her tongue follow the pathway and lapped at the shallow insides of the hole, her sensitive tastebuds picking up tones of citrus that reminded her of the enemas her very first Ass lover had used, way back when they were still in Enhancement Phase. But Carolina hadn't had these Enhancements. Ass's sphincters—she seemed to have at least seven—were pumping Mouth's tongue, sucking her in. "Please," Ass cried, and Mouth guessed the now-thin sliver of ice was pushing up against and stimulating other Enhancements further inside.

"Is the ice still there?" Mistress Azur asked suspiciously.

"It is, please Mistress, please I promise, but it's melting, please may I come for you, oh oh oh—"

Ass's pungency was ripe and earthy, and Mouth's olfactory and gustatory nerves were sending desperate signals to her brain about the necessity of coming, sooner rather than later. She ignored them and tried to focus on matching the rhythm of Ass's backward thrusts, working her tongue harder, faster, deeper. She was rewarded with a fresh round of "oh-oh-oh-oh-oh!" from Ass. The last bit of ice puddled to water, but Mouth decided to keep going, hoping that Ass might not notice or in any case would not complain. "Plee-ee-ee-ee-ease!" screamed Ass, her voice cracking with desperation and need, which apparently pleased the Mistresses.

"Now," said Mistress Azur, and Ass came, releasing a honey-lavender secretion and convulsing around Mouth's tongue in a series of contractions so powerful that it took every ounce of Mouth's willpower to stop her own orgasm.

She pulled out, exhausted, and sat back on her knees. Ass turned around and sat next to her, and they leaned on each other for a moment. Mouth was surprised at how emotional she felt toward Ass: proud and tender and grateful all at the same time. She rested her head on Ass's shoulder and closed her eyes.

"Thank you, Mistresses," Ass said softly, after a moment.

Mouth sat up and opened her eyes. "Thank you, 'istresses," she echoed, meaning it. Mistress Azur caught her eye and grinned, then blew her a slow sultry kiss that made Mouth flush all over, hungering to feel those long soft fingers, not just air, caressing her lips.

☣

Cunt's extravagant vulva was only the surface of a series of gorgeous nymphae that unfolded, layer after countless layer. As Mouth thrust the ice inward, following it with her tongue, she felt like a deep-sea diver entering the world's most intricate sea anemone. When the crystals in her lips touched the ones embedded in Cunt's labia, electric impulses of pleasure surged through her entire body—and Cunt's, too, by the sound of her moans and pleas. There was plenty of ice, so Mouth left it protruding and moved upward to Cunt's prominent clitoris, swirling round and round it with her tongue, then seizing it with her whole mouth and pressing lightly with her teeth. Cunt was begging, thrusting, pleading, screaming about her need to orgasm, but Mistress Azur just laughed.

"No, no," she said, and Mouth heard that gleeful little clap again, "this is far too much fun! Let's not let her come, darling?"

Will must have agreed, and Mouth could tell that if she continued tongue-fucking Cunt's clitoris—now swollen to almost twice its size, looking more like a diamond-studded cervix than a clit—the poor submissive would be unable to help herself. She didn't want to get Cunt in trouble, so she pulled back and went searching through Cunt's delicious folds for the orifice again. Her tongue found the ice-rod, greatly diminished, and maneuvered it upward to where she thought Cunt's g-spot would be. Cunt's moans grew increasingly guttural, the ice shrunk to barely a sliver, and still the Mistresses seemed determined to deny Cunt her pleasure. Mouth wondered what the punishment would be for coming without permission. Should she try to force an orgasm anyway, to ensure her own reward sooner rather than later?

Within seconds, the question was moot, as Cunt screamed "Architecture" and then a flood spurted all over Mouth's face. She pulled out and shook her head in surprise; Cunt's briny juices had even gotten in her eyes, and she wiped them with the back of her hand before sitting back.

Will was on her feet, and furious.

"How dare you," she said, standing over Cunt. Cunt, still shuddering from the giant orgasm, began to sob and apologize all at once.

"I'm sorry Mistress, Mistresses, oh, I'm so sorry," she sputtered.

"Mouth, move," Will ordered without looking at her, and Mouth crawled away, barely remembering to take the ice bucket with her. She was overstimulated, high from smelling and swallowing both Ass's and Cunt's juices, and terrified by the tone in Will's voice, which continued, "That is *not* the appropriate use of a safeword. How dare you use a precaution designed to care for your well-being to justify your own woeful lack of self-control!"

"Mistress, I couldn't help—" Cunt began again.

"Shut up, you disobedient slut," Will said. "My dear Aurora, how are we going to punish this misbehavior?"

"How does she respond to pain?" Mistress Azur asked.

☣

Mouth relaxed back against the loveseat and cuddled next to Ass. She tried to meet Cunt's gaze, to show she hadn't deliberately set the other submissive up for failure. But Cunt's eyes darted between the two tops as Will replied to Mistress Azur: "She likes pain. It makes her come even faster." Ass smiled, and Mouth couldn't help grinning a little, too; apparently, they could both relate.

"Ah well then," Mistress Azur said, sounding slightly relieved, "that certainly won't do. Come here then, Ass."

Mouth watched as Will and Mistress Azur quickly designed a tableau for Cunt's punishment: Cunt was on her knees, hands bound behind her by a length of rope that hooked to the ceiling. Her face was buried in Ass's lovely crack, while her own asshole was plowed by Mistress Azur wielding the largest of several dildos that Will had pulled from a drawer and offered her. Neither end would give Cunt much satisfaction, as her gorgeous vulva was dangling untouched; nor could she control her own movements. A few drops of moisture dripped from Cunt's pussy onto the floor. Mouth was captivated by the sight of Mistress Azur's soft breasts heaving as she plunged the dildo in and out of Cunt's asshole, ran her short fingernails along the submissive's back and smiled wickedly when Cunt writhed at her touch.

Will grabbed one of Mouth's nipples and pulled hard, twisting her away from the scene and settling back on the loveseat. Will pushed her down toward the largest and loveliest member that Mouth had ever had the pleasure to know. It never failed to delight her, as well as scare her a little by its size: fully erect, it was at least twelve inches, three inches around, in the same lustrous olive color as the rest of Will's skin. Tonight she had a new challenge: how was she going to fit both the ice-dildo and the giant penis inside her?

Mouth reached for the now mostly melted ice bucket, but thankfully, Will shook her head no. Apparently only the submissives needed ice to break them. So Mouth placed her hands behind her neck, as she knew Will preferred, and began licking the bulbous, mushroom-shaped head with swift, spiraling strokes. Will grabbed the back of Mouth's head and thrust. Suddenly she had more dick than she could handle. She relaxed her jaw to open wider, and was rewarded with the first drops of Will's fluid on the Enhanced taste glands in the very back of her throat, specially biodesigned to savor semen or simulated semen. Mouth grunted with pleasure as she sucked the wonderfully bitter-slick pre-cum from Will's tip. She didn't care about the blood pounding in her head from lack of air; this fullness was the sensation she craved most, and if she had been able, she would herself have been pleading for an orgasm.

She could hear Cunt's frustrated moans and Ass's mounting cries. Will pounded into Mouth's throat deeply, again and again. Just as Mistress Azur ordered Ass to come, Will ejaculated, bucking so hard that Mouth was thrust back several inches, and had to catch herself with her hands on the floor. "Don't swallow," Will said just in time, so she tilted her head back, kept her lips open, closed her throat and let the thick warm nectar bathe her swollen tastebuds.

Her mouth felt hot, fiery, as though her cells had been compensating for each round of ice by generating more and more heat. She rested for a moment, back arched, eyes closed, and when she opened them she could see the rearrangement of positions. The party was like a perverted game of musical chairs, she thought, except some people didn't get chairs. For some reason she found this idea hilarious, and started laughing, then sputtered and choked on her mouthful of cum. Will came and pounded her on the back and wiped her lips with the hem of the black tunic, leaving white streaks on the fabric and an intense tingling in Mouth's lips. "OK now?"

Mouth nodded, sobering up a little, though she still felt high. The room seemed very bright. Her whole body was pulsing with need, and her hole felt raw, hot, and terribly empty. She felt fragile, and wondered in a detached way, as if at a great distance from herself, whether she was going to cry. "I' sorry I didn't kee' the cu' in 'y 'outh, 'istress," she said, but she had no idea if she was intelligible. Will pulled Mouth up onto her lap and let her rest against her shoulder. "Thank you, 'istress," Mouth murmured, eyes closed, and felt Will stroke her cheek gently. She let herself drift in a sea of sensation.

☣

When she felt Will pulling her hands behind her back, Mouth opened her eyes. Will thrust her forward with a hand between the shoulderblades so that her breasts jutted toward Mistress Azur, now sitting on the loveseat next to them. Cunt was still tonguing Ass's opening, and Ass had apparently been given license to orgasm and was doing so over and over again. Cunt was not; clearly, she was going to pay for that first orgasm for a long time.

Then Mouth forgot all about poor Cunt as Mistress Azur turned and leaned in toward her, blowing sweet breath, laced with cardamom and cloves, onto her lips. Mouth shivered, and Mistress Azur laughed. "Are you enjoying the party, my little Mouth?" Mistress Azur asked.

"Yes, 'istress," Mouth said. She wondered whether the beautiful, girlish woman was a cunt, ass, or cock.

"Say the whole sentence," Mistress Azur pouted, for all the world like a spoiled schoolgirl. She all but stamped her foot.

"Yes thank you 'istress, it's a 'ery nice 'arty," Mouth said quickly, and was rewarded by a cruel, pleased smile.

"Do you hear that, Will?" Mistress Azur said. "We throw an airy nice arty." Will laughed, and Mistress Azur continued her interview. "And are you very sleepy, my little Mouth?"

Mouth shook her head. "No, 'istress, I' not slee'y."

"Ah, but your jaw must ache, at least a little."

As she said it, Mouth realized it was true. "Yes, 'istress, 'y jaw does ache, 'ut—" she paused, not knowing if she was allowed to do more than answer the direct question. Mistress Azur nodded, so she continued. "I 'ant to 'lease you, 'istress."

"Ahh, such a sweet little slut," Mistress Azur said. "You will please me, don't worry. Now just relax. You don't have to do anything right now, understand?" Mistress Azur stroked her cheek softly.

"I think so, 'istress," Mouth said, a little confused by the sudden gentleness.

Mistress Azur ran her fingers along Mouth's lips, circling each of the six neuro-crystals in turn before tapping it directly, which caused Mouth's nerve endings to fire wildly. A mouth's standard Enhancement at puberty involved two neuro-crystals: one on the upper lip, one on the lower. They served as focal points for the pleasure nerves of the body, as well as for easy gender identification. The crystals were the last phase of Enhancement, and once you received them, your gender was set and you wore a mouth covering at all times in public. Mouth remembered her own "graduation" fondly; although she had been wearing a veil for months before, she felt a special thrill on the day she *had* to wear it.

Years later, when she'd been hired at the Executive and learned the exact amount of her new salary, she had gone out and bought the four new additions on credit. They had been well worth the eight months of reduced rations it had taken her to pay them off. "These are very pretty," Mistress Azur said, tapping them again, watching Mouth writhe. "Very sexy."

"Th-thank you, 'istress," Mouth managed, though she was nearly nonverbal with longing. Her crystals had never been teased so deliberately, and on the heels of what felt like hours of delayed gratification, her synapses were about to go into overload.

But Mistress Azur was not done. "Show me your tongue," she said.

Mouth poked the tip of it between her lips. Mistress Azur grabbed it between two fingernails and pulled, sending a wave of pain ricocheting to Mouth's brain and forcing a loud "aah" from her throat, which Mistress Azur ignored.

"Two extensions of the intrinsic muscles, I think, and—let's see— one, two, three tongue crystals?"

Mouth nodded, gasping. A typical mouth's tongue had no extensions, just the severance of the frenulum that gave the illusion of greater length. Mouth's expensive tongue, when fully unfurled, was about twice as long as an un-Enhanced tongue. Over the years, lovers had given her the extra neuro-crystals: one at the tip, useful for stimulating deep inside an ass; one in the center, which added pleasure to almost every kind of licking, from lollipops to pussies; and one in the back for deep-throating. Will had paid for that one, and used her over and over in the first weeks afterward, plunging deeply and joking that Mouth had to "make payments" for the jewel. Mouth was only too happy for the trade.

Apparently done with her inspection, Mistress Azur let go of Mouth's tongue, leaving it to dangle limply before Mouth recovered her senses enough to draw it back in. "Now I'm going to fuck you," Mistress Azur said. "You are not to lick, kiss, suck, bite, or do anything at all with your fancy little Enhanced twat. You are my hole, nothing more. Is that clear?"

"Yes 'istress," Mouth said. She was breathing hard with anticipation.

"Get on the floor and close your eyes. Hands behind your neck."

Mouth scrambled out of Will's lap to obey, eager to find out at last where Mistress Azur's pleasure center was. She had not realized it, but knowing a lover's gender was so basic, so key to understanding how to please her, that being deprived of that information made Mouth feel even more helpless. She kneeled, blind, genitals wide open, breathing. If she was to be a hole, Mistress Azur most likely was a cock, she thought; although with various double-ended pleasure toys, asses and cunts could fuck a mouth quite nicely, too.

She heard a rustling in front of her, on the floor. Perhaps Mistress shedding some clothes? But what she felt next surprised her: the Mistress licking the outer corners of Mouth's lips.

Kissing between casual sex partners, while not taboo, was unusual, especially with a Mouth. Even after more than a year of trysts, Will rarely kissed her on the lips, except as a kind of tease over her veil.

But Mistress Azur was kissing her lips directly now. Here was a new kind of torture, more sadistic than clamps or slaps: not to obey every cell in her body demanding that she respond to such direct stimulation. She was a hole, she told herself firmly; my Mistress's fuckhole. She would endure this foreplay, she would not come, she would obey. *I a' 'y 'istress's 'uck hole,* some even more submissive part of her brain echoed.

Mistress Azur slipped her tongue inside Mouth's lips and explored the gumline, running her tongue over the bottom teeth, the top teeth, pausing at the sensitive t-spot and lapping it until Mouth was moaning aloud, clenching and unclenching her fists behind her neck, even thrusting her pelvis forward, as if that would somehow help. It wasn't her turn to come, not until Mistress Azur had, but if this kept up she was going to find herself in poor Cunt's position.

But Mistress Azur moved on; that is, in. Deeper. As her lips enveloped Mouth's entire opening, something sparked, and Mouth opened her eyes with shock. Mistress Azur's mouth was locked over hers, and she was staring right into Mouth's eyes, waiting for her to process the sensation. Mistress Azur had neuro-crystals embedded, not on the outside of her lips, but just inside: a dozen of them, at least, judging from the way Mouth's own crystals were going crazy.

Mistress Azur was a mouth.

Mouth had no opportunity to consider this further, because suddenly her hole was full, and being ravaged more exquisitely than ever before. Mistress Azur's tongue penetrated deeply and then rolled upward to scrape Mouth's hypersensitive palate. The foreign tongue seemed to have numerous little crystals hidden on its undersurface. And then it felt as though two tongues were in her, twisting around, now grabbing her tongue and tugging at it, now prodding at her taste-glands. One part of the split tongue went deep into her throat and seemed to widen and grow there, almost to the size of a long narrow cock. The other curled upward and jostled her t-spot. The Mistress fucked her until she was sobbing, and then, just as Mouth was sure she could stand it no longer, she felt a flood of warm saliva fill her. Her first thought was that she had come without permission, but then she tasted it— cardamom, cloves—and realized the Mistress had ejaculated in her mouth.

Mistress Azur withdrew her tongue—tongues?—what *was* she? with a slow, torturous, spiraling motion. Mouth looked down, hypnotized, as one half of the Mistress's tongue lightly licked Mouth's lower lip and the other licked her upper lip, teasing her even as it left her empty, gaping, needing. The tongues came together and returned to Mistress Azur's mouth, which now expressed a relaxed, rather smug smile.

Mouth found she could hardly breathe, let alone speak. Her breath was shallow and loud; her heartbeat was louder still. Drool and cum dripped from her lower lip, and she was powerless to stop it, fearing that one more lick, even a slight motion of her tongue, would send her soaring across the threshold. She felt a wetness on her cheeks, and realized tears were streaming from her eyes. As if from a great distance she heard someone else begging to cum, permission being granted; the unmistakable sounds of orgasm filled the room once more. Mouth closed her eyes, and Mistress Azur took her in her arms.

After a moment—too brief—Mistress Azur shook Mouth off, stood up, smoothed her dress, and took her seat on the sofa again. Mouth looked up at her: how beautiful she was. Her full lips were moist and swollen, but without the telltale crystals on the outside, no one could have identified her as a mouth, even now. The logical part of Mouth wanted to ask how, and what kinds of Enhancements these were, and how Mistress Azur had been allowed to wear them concealed, and if there were others like her. The logical part, though, was in control of less than 2% of Mouth's functioning right now. The other 98% was purely hormonal, and screaming for release.

"Thank me," said Mistress Azur. She was watching Mouth with keen, dark eyes. "And tell me how that felt to you."

Mouth arched her back trying to get enough air in her lungs for a deep breath, trying to calm herself enough to reassemble phonemes into words, sentences. She had no idea what she would say until she heard herself blurt out, "I lo' you, 'istress."

Mistress Azur raised an eyebrow. "Does she love everyone who fucks her silly?" she asked Will.

"She's never said it to me," Will said, laughing. "You must have made an impression, my dear."

Mouth felt humiliated, but she did not regret her passionate words, even as Mistress Azur looked at her and said coolly, "What an interesting creature." The mistress smiled slightly, as if enjoying a private joke. Mouth felt pinned by her eyes, unable to move or look away, and wanting only to stay locked in that gaze forever.

Will said, "It's your turn now, Mouth. Which of us would you like to decide how you get to come?"

Mistress Azur turned away—a mercy, since it broke the trance. Mouth lowered her eyes and tried to think. After being denied decisions all evening, it was confusing to be asked to choose now. Her heart and nerve endings all wanted Mistress Azur, there was no question about it; but she felt a loyalty toward Will.

"'lease 'istresses, 'atever you decide?" she tried.

Will leaned down and slapped Mouth's right cheek, hard. Mistress Azur followed suit with her left.

"We *decided* to give you a choice, my precious Mouth," Mistress Azur said, and Mouth's heart leaped at her use of the possessive. *Yes, I am yours*, something in her said, something that realized that in all of her years of submission, she had only been play-acting. *Own me*, she wanted to say.

But Will was staring at her. "Hurry up and choose," she said finally. "You're not the only slut here we need to supervise."

Mouth didn't want Will to think badly of her; actually, she felt incredibly grateful to Will for all the times they had shared together, and for inviting her tonight in the first place. "'lease 'istress 'ill," she said finally, and Will patted her lap.

Mouth climbed up, suddenly eager. A good finger-fucking by Will and the release of an orgasm would be just what she needed to get her emotions under control.

But as Will positioned her—sitting sideways again, hands twisted into prayer position behind her back, breasts thrust forward—Mouth found she was looking directly at Mistress Azur. Again, she couldn't tear her eyes away from that dark, intense gaze; oh, and those full, ripe lips... which came closer. And then she was in heaven, because Mistress Azur was kissing her again. Could this even be called kissing? She didn't know; it was more intense than any kind of fucking she had ever experienced. Then the Mistress pulled back.

"I'm guessing she could come right this second," Mistress Azur said. "Is that right, little Mouth?"

Mouth nodded, not trusting herself to speak.

"Speak," Mistress Azur said with a slap. Her cheek stung.

"Yes 'istress, I could co' right this second," Mouth said, feeling the indignity of her situation, wanting to stop speaking like an imbecile, or at least to close her lips so at least she wouldn't be drooling like one. And in the same moment she realized that Mistress Azur had uncovered the core of her: an open mouth, craving, hungering, praying to be fucked. She had been lubricating for hours, she could taste the cum of every person in the room mingling together in her orifice, and the production of saliva and precum from her own glands was far, far beyond her own control. The truth was, nothing was in her control. Everything she was, every part of her sex, her self, was being controlled by the Mistresses. It was unbearable; she was the luckiest girl in the world.

And by the looks on their faces, the Mistresses knew it. Oh, they were very pleased with themselves; they would draw out this moment for their own satisfaction. The last resistance in Mouth melted away; she would give them everything they wanted, she would beg and plead and submit to their whims, their capriciousness and their cruelty.

"'lease, 'istresses," she said, trying to put all this into words, "'lease 'ay I co' for you?"

"We're not even touching her," Mistress Azur observed. In fact, they were: Will's hand was on her neck, firmly controlling her movements, while Mistress Azur had just begun idly fondling Mouth's nipples through the latex. She was trapped between them, but they were not touching her genitals at all. It didn't matter. She was so aroused; all she needed was permission.

"Will says you like pain," Mistress Azur mused, tossing her locks back and flicking a sharp blue fingernail at Mouth's now-erect nipple. "Would you like a bit of pain with your orgasm, my precious Mouth?"

Oh, yes, please, anything just as long as you keep calling me yours, Mouth thought, since you own me already, every part of me... Aloud she said, "Yes 'lease, if it 'leases you, 'istress." Mistress Azur smiled.

"When I pinch your nipple like this," she said with a sudden, fierce twist that made Mouth cry out, "you will come. Not before. You will come as many times as I choose, at the precise moments I choose. Do you understand?"

"Yes 'istress, I 'ill—" Mouth began, and was cut off by Mistress Azur's lips covering hers. For a moment there was nothing else, no intrusion, no tongue-caresses: just this enclosure, this place of hot, erotic safety; this home.

The hard twist of her nipple surprised her, and she came as commanded, a small powerful orgasm flooding her mouth with her own cum, the taste as familiar to her as skin. Instinctively she tried to pull back, but Will's grip was firm at the back of her neck. She had no choice but to submit to Mistress Azur's rough exploration of her throbbing organ. Mistress Azur lapped up Mouth's cum while making mmm-mmm sounds. *Devour me*, Mouth would have thought, if she'd been able to form words.

Then she started fucking Mouth, hard. The divided tongue, the dozens of neuro-crystals, all had Mouth ready for an orgasm again within mere seconds, and she tried to plead with moans and sounds.

Her nipple twisted, and again the flood came. It happened over and over, without pause or rest in between convulsions, until Mouth felt lightheaded, losing all track of time, all count, all knowledge of her name or where she was; she was only this mouth, being so thoroughly ravaged, and this nipple that—ow! aaahhh—surely was about to be ripped off entirely, it hurt so much. A few times she felt Mistress Azur's cum flow into her too, and she swallowed ecstatically, savoring the warm ambrosia all the way down her throat. Mistress Azur left no part of her orifice unexplored; each of Mouth's precious neuro-crystals was given its own orgasm. The Mistress bit lightly at the crystal at the tip of Mouth's tongue, then sucked on it, scraping her own labial neuro-crystals against it, hurting it more than Mouth would have thought possible, until the biting started again, when the previous layer of pain became just a dream. Pain and pleasure escalated each other, and her nipple was abused harshly again and again. Mouth came, and came, and came until she blacked out.

☣

She woke on a bed, cool water at her lips. She sputtered, realized she was incredibly thirsty, and tried to sit up. Ass, stripped of her latex outfit, offered Mouth a dipperful from the now-melted ice bucket. It happened to be dangling from Ass's little penis, rather painfully by the look of it. Mouth propped herself up on her elbows and drank gratefully from the dipper that Ass held to her lips. "You look so fuckable right now," Ass said, smiling sweetly.

Mouth grinned back. "You, too." She glanced around. "Are we allowed—" The Mistresses were on the far side of the room, crouched over something—probably Cunt—and she heard moans coming from that direction.

"Yes," said Ass. "After your little 'icebreaker,' it's a regular orgy now. You and I were allowed out of our jumpsuits and allowed to come whenever. Cunt's still being punished for her mistake."

Mouth looked down and realized she was indeed naked. Someone had stripped her and even covered her with a blanket. She tried to bend her knees, and realized she was bound spread-eagle to the bed by her ankles.

"I guess I'm not going anywhere," she said. "But—oh my gosh. Poor Cunt. I feel so bad. I wasn't trying to make her come without permission, but—"

"Are you kidding?" Ass said. "We've been together for thirteen years, and I can guarantee you this is the best night of her whole fucking life."

Cunt apparently agreed, because her pleading moans at the other end of the room escalated into high-pitched shrieks, followed by a series of deep grunts and then a fervent round of "Thank you Mistresses oh Thank you finally oh god oh my god Thank you Thank you!" Mouth suddenly remembered she wasn't supposed to speak normally, and she blushed, quickly parting her lips.

Ass noticed, and laughed. "Don't worry, sweet Mouth, I won't tell," she said. "I know what you did for me, even though the ice was melted. I owe you one." Then she reached down and traced Mouth's opening with a finger as Mouth shuddered, aroused again.

The rest of the party passed in a blur. From time to time someone came over to use her mouth, and in between, she dozed to the pleasant soundtrack of fucking. Cunt stopped by to straddle her face, saying, "No hard feelings, darling." After they both came, Mouth smiled at her tenderly, sleepily.

Mistress Azur came to her, too, and tied her arms to the bedposts before leaving sharp little bite-marks all over her body. Mouth cherished each jolt of pleasure-pain, hoping they were deep enough to leave marks for a few days. When she was a quivering mass of need, Mistress Azur moved upward and nibbled at her lips, then roughly deep-throated her to two quick blissful orgasms. Mouth could taste all the others on the Mistress's breath: Ass's honey-lavender-citrus scent, Cunt's sea anemone flavors, the bitter seed from Will that set her throat pulsing. When she withdrew, Mouth gazed at her glassy-eyed, and said again, so that there would be no mistake, "I lo' you, 'istress." Mistress Azur met her gaze with an inscrutable expression, and answered with a sweet, lingering kiss that followed Mouth into a light, floating dream.

Finally Will came over to say that everyone was staying over, since it was too late to send them out on the Tube, and did Mouth want to stay where she was or be untied? Mouth loved the safe comfortable feeling of the bondage, so Will loosened just one arm slightly; she would be able to free herself in an emergency, but could stay just as she was. The lights were lowered, and she slept deeply.

☣

The next thing she knew, Mistress Azur's tongue was inside her again, fucking her awake. Had she slept next to Mouth? Mouth kissed her back passionately, trying to open her throat and suck the Mistress's tongue—tongues!—at the same time, and was rewarded by Mistress Azur's sweet, spicy spurting. A twist of her sore nipple, and Mouth came too, wide awake and aware of how raw she felt.

"Good morning, sleepyhead," Mistress Azur said. "Everyone else is already up."

"Good 'orning, 'istress," Mouth said shyly, memories of the wild evening flooding back in a rush, making her flush.

"Speak properly now," Mistress Azur said, a little briskly. "That's going to get annoying soon. And you don't have to call me Mistress any more."

Mouth was crushed. Tears sprang to her eyes, and she bit down on her lip to keep from crying, focusing on the cold harsh pain. Of course, she was just a plaything to Mistress—to Azur. It was stupid to expect an orgy to end in… well. In love.

Mouth felt extremely, profoundly, humiliatingly stupid, and furiously set about freeing herself from Will's ties.

Mistress Azur remained seated on the edge of the bed. Mouth wished the woman, who suddenly seemed like a stranger again, would go away and let her have her breakdown in semi-privacy. Instead, Mistress Azur watched her intently. Untied, Mouth felt more naked than she could bear, and wrapped the blanket around her.

"Mouth," Mistress Azur said.

"My name is Laura," Mouth said, but it sounded like a lie.

"Mouth," Mistress Azur insisted. "Look at me."

Mouth forced herself to meet the other woman's gaze, though she had to look away almost immediately.

"I think you've misunderstood me," Mistress Azur said. "I meant that you don't have to call me Mistress anymore, if you don't want to. The obligation connected to the party is over. If you do want to—well, I would be very flattered. You are—" She paused, lowering her voice. "As the Mistress of the party, it was my responsibility to spread my attention around, and everyone here contributed to a wonderful evening. But you: You are simply the most amazing woman I have ever had the honor to meet."

Mouth was speechless.

"And to fuck, of course," Mistress Azur said, smiling, so Mouth smiled too. Her whole body was tingling now, from her teeth to her toes, not with arousal but with something even more profound: joy.

"And," the mistress continued, "I think *love* is a very strong word."

Mouth felt fragile, ready to break. It was too much to process, she couldn't understand… "So I'd like you to know me a bit better before you decide if you want to say it again. Is that ok?"

Mouth nodded. *Of course. Anything you say is ok.* A tear began its slow, saline roll down the side of her nose.

"Do you have anywhere you have to be today?" Mistress Azur asked.

Mouth shook her head. She could not have said what date it was, or perhaps even what month, but she knew she had left the day clear so that she could recover and enjoy the after-buzz of the party.

"Would you like to come home with me?"

Mouth nodded. There was nothing she could imagine wanting more.

The teardrop trembled at the corner of her lip.

"May I touch you?" Mistress Azur asked.

Mouth almost laughed aloud. After giving so much, such a simple request—but it was, after all, a beginning.

She assented. Azur reached out and, with one finger, wiped away the tear. Then she touched the fingertip to her tongue, savoring its salt.

"You are even more yummy than you looked," she said, smiling.

"Thank you, Mistress," Mouth said, finally finding her voice. And then, boldly: "So are you."

Azur laughed out loud. Mouth caught a spark in the mistress's eye—one of her own lip-crystals, reflected back. And she laughed too, letting all her questions and worries rest. There was so much to say, and at the same time nothing that needed to be said at all; and they had all day, maybe the rest of their lives, to say it in.

The Remaker

Fabio Fernandes

1. WHAT'S IN A NAME

Menard. His name is Pierre Menard.

This isn't his birth name. It doesn't matter, it really doesn't make any difference—what should anyone care about such a trifling thing these days?

Besides, nobody even knows if he really existed. For the person who signs this name, such a discussion is immaterial.

How do I know that?

Pierre Menard killed me.

☣

As far as a fairly thorough research in the Hive can show you, there were quite a handful of men who went by the name Pierre Menard in recorded history.

One of the first Menards I've been able to trace down was a Canadian businessman and fur trader who lived in the early 1800s. He was presiding officer of the Illinois Territorial Legislature and from 1818 to 1822 served as its first lieutenant governor.

The second one was a musician. Pierre Menard, American violinist and concertmaster for The Neon Philharmonic, a psychedelic pop band formed in 1967. They released only two albums before the group disbanded in 1975.

(There's another Pierre Menard still, also a violinist, who played in the Vermeer Quartet and who died of AIDS in 1994. I couldn't find out if he was the same guy of the Neon Philharmonic, though somehow it doesn't seem so—but it's a creepy coincidence all the same.)

There was also a Dr. Pierre Menard, anesthesiologist, in Logan, West Virginia. But I couldn't find much about him except for the fact that he was actively working until the early 2010s. He may be still alive today.

As well as the last namesake of my list. A Pierre Menard whose vestiges, no matter how hard I tried, I could never find. Not until the day I died.

☣

Pierre Menard, Author of the Quixote, is one of the most important short stories of the twentieth century. In this story, written in the form of an academic paper by Argentinean writer Jorge Luis Borges, the author poses as a reviewer who analyzes the work of a recently deceased French writer who, among other literary exploits, wrote *Don Quixote*.

To be more specific, according to Borges, Menard's subterranean work "consists of the ninth and thirty-eighth chapters of the first part of Don Quixote and a fragment of chapter twenty-two."

The thing is, Pierre Menard didn't only *rewrite* Cervantes's classic work. He wrote it as if Cervantes had *never* done it. But it's not an alternate history story, for, in that universe, Cervantes *had written* Don Quixote—exactly the same way we know he did, and using the very words he used.

Menard just applied the seat of his pants to the seat of the chair, as people said then, and wrote the aforementioned chapters. No strings attached, no computer tricks: Borges wrote that story in 1939, just before Alan Turing and Bletchley Park, a time when *computers* were simply the name given to the mathematicians performing calculations in notebooks (paper ones) and chalkboards (dumb, non-interactive ones).

His method, according to Borges, was quite simple: "Know Spanish well, recover the Catholic faith, fight against the Moors or the Turk, forget the history of Europe between the years 1602 and 1918, be Miguel de Cervantes."

Borges was evidently making fun of the then new canons of modernity, the death of the author, and other notions that were foreign to him, a man born in Argentina but partially raised in Switzerland and strongly immersed in the European culture. It is one of his best stories.

His Menard was a complete fiction. The other, however, was very real: he killed me in 2026.

2. THE FIRST BOOK OF MENARD

This other Menard was what I called a *remaker*. As his famous fictional namesake, he rewrote books. Not just chapters or fragments, as the original Menard did (even if he did it only in the imagination of Borges).

No. My Menard rewrote *entire novels*.

This should come as no surprise for anyone these days, considering you can squirt entire libraries into a nanoimplant and copy/paste them as you see fit—a procedure far older than the digital pundits would make you believe, using techniques not unknown to the Dada and the Surrealists, the Founding Fathers of altered books in the 1910s and 1920s. What is the big deal about a person who rewrites stories, since the very notion of *rewriting* was challenged so many years ago and now seems such an effortless thing?

That, I thought then, was the keyword. *Effort*. Why should anyone even try to rewrite a novel and then publish it in paper as if it was an original work? And, weirder yet, *without letting anyone know*?

Why did I care?

⚕

When you are a researcher, you can't afford not to care about such things. You are compelled to search—not a futile, useless search for its own sake, but a search for answers. The questions may vary, but they are always there, hovering over the mind of the researcher. Because there will always be questions.

The first question that made my path cross with Menard's was, evidently: *why?*

My original question was entirely other—and I'm a bit ashamed now by the fact that I can't even remember what it was. I was in the university's library, browsing the bookshelves, another purpose in mind.

I had the entire space of the library all to myself. Almost nobody goes there anymore. Not after the last round of education reforms and the end of live classes. The university offers all its books in digital format through the Hive, and students don't even bother coming to the campus now.

There is only a skeletal staff to keep things clean and tidy in the old buildings, plus the occasional researcher who likes the peace and quiet of the place. But only oldsters like me still come. The younger ones would rather be at home or coffee shops, STing from there.

Sometimes I felt like Wells' Traveller in the distant future, alone in a library full of swirling dust motes, touching crumbling books. But sometimes the bizarre image of Sean Connery in *Zardoz* also came to mind, a violent savage with braided hair wearing only red shorts, running down narrow aisles full of books and empty of people. Both images were sad to me.

It was on one of these lonely browsings that I found the First Book.

I still didn't know then if that was the first book he ever wrote; I called it so because it was the very first that I found. It became easier to me to call it so, and it was as good a method as any.

The book was an old hardcover edition of *1984*. But it didn't have a dust jacket, so it took some time for me to register the fact that it was Orwell's classic novel. I also took a very long time to notice that the author's name on the spine wasn't Orwell's.

I looked at it and couldn't find anything wrong with that. It was just after I began leafing through the pages that I closed it suddenly and went to the cover.

It read:

Pierre Menard

1984

No publisher name.

My first reaction was to start reading the book right there. I was sure then that it was a kind of parody or satire. (Anthony Burgess, for example, had written such a story in 1978—but he named it *1985*, and it was intended as a tribute to Orwell's classic novel. It was a completely different story.)

But the beginning—ah, the beginning:

It was a bright cold day in April, and the clocks were striking thirteen. Winston Smith, his chin nuzzled into his breast in an effort to escape the vile wind, slipped quickly through the glass doors of Victory Mansions, though not quickly enough to prevent a swirl of gritty dust from entering along with him.

I went on reading. The rest of the book, as much as memory served, was exactly the same as George Orwell had written. Word for word.

My second reaction was laughter.

I found it amusing that someone could give her/himself the trouble to do this kind of prank those days. It reminded me of the works of the Italian collective Luther Blissett, later known as Wu-Ming. They had done some really good tactical media actions between the end of twentieth century and the beginning of the twenty-first.

My third reaction was to get the book and take it home with me. It was too much fun to dismiss it.

It was a refreshing, sunny thought in my day. I couldn't help but laugh, still standing there in the aisle, surrounded by the dust-filled surviving books in the university library. There was no one there to shush me.

3. THE AGE OF REFERENCE

Is it possible to be alone in a crowd these days?

Of course it is. Everybody is alone these days.

São Paulo in 2026 is a huge river, an Amazon of people, a Joycean riverrun, a band of Blooms blooming around, germinating thoughts on the run and in the sidewalks, everybody talking aloud, apparently to themselves, alone or to someone else via their implants.

When cellphones became obsolete, the only way was to become molecular. So they crammed huge computational power in bioware or smart jewelry and created SelfTalking. STing involves mainly talking to personal AIs—mostly limited, rather dumb AIs, but who cares? At least they do what they are told to, no complaining, no need to pay anything but a ridiculously cheap microfee per month.

And they remind you of your chores—that is, the chores they are too dumb or non-mobile enough to do for you; they can store messages, write and/or record messages, locate places, find your contacts wherever you happen to be walking by, ping them to let them know where you are (or block them so they don't), arrange for orders and pay in advance whenever you enter a café or a supermarket. They can even talk to others for you so you don't have to.

Sometimes I enjoy standing apart from the crowd, in the intersection of Rua Augusta and Avenida Paulista, under the concrete marquise of the huge building of the Conjunto Nacional. I usually take with me an extra-large foam cup of steaming hot caramel machiatto or cinnamon latte from the Starbucks across the street and just stand there, sipping the warm beverage leisurely, watching people walking or riding by.

That was exactly what I was doing a couple of months ago, right after finding the First Book of Menard. I was chilling out, book under my arm, doing nothing, when a soft ping in my inner ear interrupted my train of thought.

"There is a white bike available just around the block, Dave," said the low-pitch male voice.

"Thanks but no thanks, Butler," I said. "You already know that, why ask?"

"You keep complaining about your legs," the AI replied. "You probably need some exercise. Riding bicycles is good for your heart and lungs, and for your varicose-"

I nodded it down, and the professorial voice dimmed away. Sometimes it's good to be by yourself. Just watching the white bikes go by.

☣

After the Big Gridlock of 2014, when virtually all of the motor vehicles in São Paulo simply got stuck in a perpetual lockout, things got very nasty.

Nobody believed it could happen. Until it happened: one evening, at rush hour, the city registered the worst bottleneck of its history: more than 540 kilometers of jammed traffic all over the city.

São Paulo was the third biggest city in the world then. It was the first to crash.

It was the worst week of my life. I got stuck in my apartment without electricity. The running water in my building went off right after that. When I had just run out of food the Martial Law was lifted, after six days of mayhem.

By then the city had hundreds of dead.

When it became clear the gridlock was serious (that is, more serious than usual), people started getting out of their cars to see what was going on. Then the fights started. First, people in the cars began to shout and curse aloud. Then, fistfights. Suddenly, someone had a gun.

And the shooting started. All over the city.

Then someone had the brilliant idea to move the cars away. Later that first day GloboNews and CNN showed some impressive footage of massive heaps of people pushing cars all along one major artery of the city, and then, when they saw it didn't make any difference—because even when they *could* move a vehicle (a Volkswagen or a Japanese car; an SUV was out of the question), they simply didn't have the leeway to move it further—they just burned the cars on the spot.

Needless to say the fires started to spread almost as fast as the bullets.

New Downtown, where Avenida Paulista is located, became a war zone—something I had until then already seen only in newscasts about Middle East or Eastern European countries.

Welcome to civilization, I told myself then. *This is the price to pay to end your childhood and become an old country.*

It took the municipality the better part of a year just to clear the city of the rusted, battered, and charred carcasses of cars. To this day, cars are banned from Greater Downtown.

Two years after the tragedy, white bicycles started to show up all over the Greater Downtown perimeter. They were just there, parked but not locked up, as if inviting everyone to take a hike.

Nobody ever found out who put them there in the first place. A blog pundit wrote that the white bikes were a direct reference to the PROVOS of Amsterdam in the 1960s, who for months effectively created a free-for-all system of transportation where all that was required of you was that you took the bike wherever you found it, used it, then left it wherever you got it. As simple as that.

Incredible as it may sound, it *was* simple. I don't know why that stuck. Maybe people were tired of allthat senseless traffic killing. But it's been almost fifteen years since the Gridlock and the white bikes endure. People became too fond of them. Me too—even though I don't use them. I'd rather walk. That's what I do the most since I retired.

☣

In this day and age, if you don't wear any kind of computational apparatus, you're severely disconnected from the world. Sometimes, especially when I'm watching the walking-and-biking crowds down Avenida Paulista, I fancy I'm offline, though I only muffle the pinging sound in my head (even though the default is already a subsonic sound I can't hear but can hardly avoid feeling, like a buzz in the teeth). I also put on hold the messages that are being squirted to me all the time.

The only concession I make to myself is to create a hotlist of 1980s music and watch the crowd passing to and fro to a soundtrack consisting of The Cure, Echo and the Bunnymen, Siouxsie and the Banshees, The Smiths, Joy Division.

But I don't flaunt my virtual absence of wearable computing. At least, not like the Unconnected do.

4. TRIBES OF THE XXI CENTURY

Occasionally, in my *flanérie* by the streets of São Paulo, I find clusters of people who really talk to *each other*. Youngsters, mostly. It's good to see them: they have a certain punk attitude you don't see every day, a healthy behavior that is necessary and more than welcome in times of conformity and cold comfort.

They usually wear dumb clothes, real used vintage material, and they wear them like a badge of honor. A couple of years ago I wrote a paper for *Science Fiction Studies* comparing the Unconnected with the non-telepaths in Alfred Bester's *The Demolished Man*. They are the pebbles that roll in the bottom of the river, below its murky depths, inhabiting the undercurrents. Invisible things, whose influence is not seen but is felt if you know just where to look.

I had interviewed one of them at the time, a well-groomed man in his thirties wearing used clothes which seemed to have come from the 1980s without the aid of a time machine, the hard way, really bought in a flea market. The guy claimed to be non-political but I couldn't help but notice a hint of a surprisingly right-wing discourse in his speech for someone who considered himself a revolutionary.

Even so, what he told me rang a bell in my mind: "You see, we work between the tentacles of the beast."

"And who would be the beast?" I asked, doing my best *agent provocateur* face.

"Why, man," he said, giving me his best derisive snort. "All you zombies."

Quoting Heinlein, of all things. Preaching to the choir. I still wonder if he knew from whom he was corydoctoring the quoting.

☣

Midori was waiting for me when I got home the evening after I found the First Book. I almost forgot I was going to cook for her that night.

She was the subject of my latest post-doc fellowship, one of the first meta-gender individuals of the world.

I met her at a symposium in Canada. She was so busy at the time that I could barely speak to her at all—even though she, just like me, lived in São Paulo.

But São Paulo is a huge city. You could roam its streets for years and never find a single friend. And the irony of it was that we had to meet in a symposium in Canada of all places—she had just finished her PhD on the pioneers of sex change and was all the rage in Brazilian academia. She gave a lecture on Christine Jorgensen and the pioneers of transsexualism.

I was fascinated. I approached her at the end of her communication and invited her for dinner. And that's how it started for us.

As soon as we returned to Brazil we started a relationship—we lived in transit, orbiting around each other, not exactly in love, but definitely in caring, in comforting, in sex. Sometimes Midori slept at my place, sometimes I slept at hers.

It was a unique experience. The Meta-Genders are a kind of 2.0 hermaphrodite: you not only change your sex, you get to keep your original genitalia as well.

Midori was born a man and since early childhood had behaved as a girl, showing all the signs of a feminine psyche. So when she was eighteen, she applied for a sex change. But her therapist told her to wait because of the new meta-gender therapies that were just being developed then. She didn't regret waiting.

By the time she was twenty-six, she underwent surgery and DNA-resetting. She had her testicles removed and a vagina grown just beneath the root of the penis.

When I met her in that symposium, she was thirty-one and a very happy person. I basked in her glow, listened to her talking in the communication sessions, and finally took the courage to invite her for a date. Since we were both foreigners and strangers to Montréal, we both had our share of fun just trying to find the best places to eat, drink, and be merry.

And boy, we *were* merry.

We still were, even after almost four years. She was the best interlocutor I've had in years, a person with whom I could talk and relate to. The first thing I did when I got home was give her the book and ask her if she could see what was wrong with it while I started preparing the pasta.

"Who is this Menard, David?" she asked from the living room sofa.

"*This* Menard I don't know yet," I said from the kitchen. "Have you ever read Jorge Luis Borges?"

"Heard of, but no, never read him."

I went to the scriptorium and fetched the Volume 1 of the Complete Works of Borges in Portuguese. I searched for the story in the index and handed it to her. "Read this," I said. "It's just six pages. You won't take long."

She read it while I finished the *puttanesca* sauce. When I served the *tagliatelle*, I asked, "Did you like it?"

She made a so-so face. "Not exactly my cup of tea, but it's good, yes... This Pierre Menard is a character created by him, isn't he?"

I smiled. "Yes, you've got the point. Borges liked this kind of reference-mixing. In fact, half the stuff he throws into the story is fake, or in the very least wasn't written by Menard, who, obviously, doesn't exist."

"But the passage about the Quixote... I didn't understand a thing. What's the point of making the guy rewrite the book word for word, with no alterations?"

"He was thumbing his nose at the modernists, that's all. Remember when he says that Cervantes wrote a thing that should be expected of him because of the times in which he lived, but not Menard. Menard was a genius because of his balls, of the courage to write something nobody would ever think to write. It was a very polite joke."

"It wasn't funny."

"Oh, it wasn't meant to be laughable," I lied. Because *I* laughed every time I read it. "He meant it to be a satirical piece, to tease the modernist writers of his time."

"But what about *this* Menard? What the fuck does he mean with that? And what for? Are you sure he didn't simply put a new cover on an old book? Why would he give himself all this trouble?"

Now, that was a good question. In fact, that was the whole point of what I was seeing now as my next post-doc research project.

Why in hell would someone do that sort of thing today?

After dinner, Midori made coffee and I took the Borges back to the scriptorium to take some notes. I opened the book and found the story again. I read it again right there, standing by my desk, and found the passage I was looking for:

Menard didn't want to compose another Quixote—which is easy—

but the Quixote itself. Needless to say, he never contemplated a mechanical transcription of the original; he did not propose to copy it. His admirable intention was to produce a few pages which would coincide—word for word and line for line—with those of Miguel de Cervantes.

I repeated every word in a quiet, almost reverent tone. Then I closed the book, put it on my desk (I would certainly be looking for it again along the next few days), and returned to the living room to enjoy a good cup of coffee with my gorgeous girlfriend.

5. THE SECOND BOOK OF MENARD

A week later, I found the second Menard book in the university library.

This time, though, I was looking for it. Actively. And, even though the library space wasn't very big, it took me an entire week to find it.

I began browsing the Classic SF Masterworks section for other copies of Menard's *1984*, as I had already done the day I found the First Book. Nothing; but that was expected.

After that, I went to the Fantastic Literature section. I fingered every single book in the several rows of shelves I had become so acquainted with in decades past. To no avail, alas.

I spent days in futile search and contemplation. It wasn't as if I had anything better to do.

On the fifth day, having arrived early and spent hours in the Classic Weird/New Weird sections, suddenly Butler told me it was half past eleven. Early, but I was hungry. I decided I would take a break and go for an Italian restaurant near the campus.

Then, as it always seems to happen when we're ready to give up on something, the corner of my eye just caught a glimpse of a gold-emblazoned *M* in a book spine in the Classic Cyberpunk section.

I backpedaled until I saw what had caught my attention.

Naked Lunch.

Only this time it wasn't an old edition. This book was a comparatively new edition—it didn't show a publication date, but it sported a colored cover with an abstract, electronic-art-like illustration. The looks, the typography, everything in it told my senses that the copy I now held in my hands was a paperback published in the 1980s or early 1990s.

But the name of the author—*Pierre Menard*—belied all that information.

I can't remember for how long I was there, mesmerized by that name on the cover (later, of course, Butler would tell me that I stayed like that for exactly 8.34 minutes. A very long time for a machine, but not for an old man. We see things differently).

I caught myself almost caressing the paperback, turning it around in my hands, sniffing the paper like a fetishist. Some do say that reading paper books today is indeed a kind of fetish.

Maybe it is, and so what? Books are almost non-existent today. That's why this thing he did was so outrageous, so surprising, so…

Marvelous.

Whoever was this Menard, a single person or a tactical group, he did it. He had the gall, he had the balls, this son-of-a-bitch.

I took the Second Book of Menard home with me. In my head, Psychedelic Furs. *Heaven.*

⚯

When Midori arrived, I was so immersed in my reading I didn't even notice her.

"How did it go today?" she asked me from the scriptorium door.

I showed her the book.

"Sonofabitch," she said, smiling.

"Exactly what I thought," I said, happy that she got it at once.

"What are you going to do next?" she said.

"I don't know yet," I admitted. I was still amazed, not sure if I really wanted to do anything.

She smiled, not without a bit of irony. "I'm amazed you still haven't written an abstract or even a whole paper about it."

She was right. That was exactly what I should have been doing.

That night, she cooked. I did the research. I told Butler to ping the RFID system of my library to search for the best books to help me with this mysterious affair. I ended up with a Babel-sized pile of books on my desk and started making notes on paper, in the time-honored way I still liked.

Until I got tired.

Method, I thought. I was getting scarce on method. I needed to do something more focused than just taking notes. I just couldn't figure out exactly what.

⚯

"What's the matter with you, my love?" Midori asked softly, later that night. I looked at her for a long time before answering, caressing her silky black hair, the curves of her body, stopping only briefly at her penis and her vagina just below it.

I massaged her clitoris tenderly with my little finger while thumb and index finger masturbated the base of her penis. It's tricky, but she taught me how to do so to please her the way she liked it best. And I always was a quick learner.

I loved to detain myself and explore that body, always so new to me. In the beginning, I liked to recite John Donne to her, the *Elegy XIX—To His Mistress Going To Bed*.

License my roving hands, and let them go
Before, behind, between, above, below.
O my America! my new-found-land.

Because that was what she was to me then. A new territory, for which I had no map—and who did?

Later, when she read the poem in its entirety, she told me I was being unconsciously homophobic—or, at the very least, an old-fashioned *machista*, because of its ending:

To teach thee, I am naked first; why than,
what needst thou have more covering than a man?

"Fuck off, sweetie," she told me in her best mischievous tone. "There is no *man* in this relationship."

Then she took me from behind and, oh, she was *so* right.

☣

Later, both of us sluggish right after lovemaking and just before falling quickly into sleep, she suggested, "Why don't you talk to Marcos to check the age of these books?"

"Good idea," I said, and fell asleep.

6. TRIBES OF THE XIX CENTURY

The following afternoon I took the subway and went to the Ophicina Typographica.

The place almost hadn't changed in twenty-odd years. Its founder and owner, designer Marcos Mello, had been a colleague of mine at the university for a brief period, where he'd taught typesetting.

I found Marcos at the iron handpress, finishing a *faux* DADA poster. I stopped for a moment to see him working, the precise mixture of extreme care and sheer muscularity he employed, first to fit each old lead type and block into the iron frame, then to lift the heavy frame into the press, and then applying the right amount of force to the lever so the paper got inked upon its entire surface in equal measure, with no blotches or smudges. That's grace under pressure for you. I loved his work.

The moment he took a break, I went to talk to him and show him the books.

"Man, this is a real superb job, very well done," he told me excitedly while examining with great care the First Book, feeling the pages with the tips of his calloused fingers, squinting at the lettering without giving pause, as if transfixed by it.

"Do you think this job could have been done today?" I asked him.

He nodded slowly, still unable to take his eyes off the book, still enraptured.

"Sure it could," he said. "It's not hard. All it takes is time and patience. You know how it is."

Indeed I knew. I had taken courses on bookbinding and typesetting with him years ago. It was a very fine and exquisite job, but also an energetic and exhausting one. I promised myself I would do it again sometime in the future, but I had no stamina for that.

He went on, explaining me how Menard could have bought reams of recycled paper and bathed then in a special tincture so it gained the appearance of a yellowing, acid paper. Of course, Marcos told me, Menard would have also stored the book in an environment proper to get fungi and dust motes, so it could smell old too.

"But where he could have done all of this?" I asked him.

He gestured around.

"In a place like this," he said. "Or even in a home press. It would take him longer, probably months if he was all by himself, but if he wasn't in a hurry…" He shrugged.

I nodded in agreement. In the early aughts, a small-press revival happened all over the world. Many writers were publishing very limited editions of their works, swimming against the stream like a bunch of happy salmon. Nobody made money out of it, but who cared?

The fad was already dead by now, but probably it wouldn't be difficult to find people in São Paulo with home presses. Marcos could help me with that. It would be fun.

☣

It was boring.

We found every small press in the city in less than an hour via the Hive. The officially listed, the unofficial ones, the *artistes*, the pirates, the pseudo-revolutionaries, the frauds.

Nobody had a clue. Some of them didn't even know who Borges was. And almost all of them had migrated definititively to the Hive and never even looked back to paper anymore—they got used to another reality.

The Internet in its previous incarnation ended in 2020.

By 2010 there were already two other terms created for orders of magnitude of data—the brontobyte and the geopbyte. Pundits doubted that anyone alive then would ever see a geopbyte hard drive.

In the end, it was no big deal. As desktop computing slowly gave way to mobile devices after 2011, the second decade of the century saw the transition from mobile to integrated. Smart clothing, thinking jewelry, implants.

Thus the Web gave way to the Hive: parallel processing in ultra-high global massive scale.

It's not the Singularity—at least not yet. There was a kind of generalized disappointment among the experts when it became clear that no Kurzweil-like spontaneous machine sentience sprouted through all that computational power. Even so, the AIs—which can admittedly pass a Turing Test, but so can a smart refrigerator today—serve us well. We can't really ask for much more than that.

I also use Butler as a messaging device. I call Pedro through it. His nick, from the ancient Web times, remains the same: *wintermute*. Like me, he is a sucker for references.

He blips into my field of vision some pictogram I don't recognize. I simply use my voice.

"Will you switch this shit off?" I said. "I want real talk for a change."

"Don't let the idiots of objectivity get you," he said, quoting Nelson Rodrigues. He knows I worked as an actor decades ago, so he quotes the most famous—and polemic—Brazilian playwright.

Pedro is one of my best never-seen-in-person friends. We are always talking online, even though he lives in São Paulo. We tried to meet for a cup of coffee two or three times, but after a while we gave up. Better have a coffee alone and talk online.

His collaborative album, *Creative Uncommons*, was one of the hits of the week through the Hive a couple of years ago, and he was the first person I considered talking to after Marcos. Marcos took care of the analog search. Pedro could help me with the digital part of it.

"It's kind of a Bizarro version of the Saint Leibowitz Order?" he asked after I explained the whole shebang to him.

"Hah. Very funny."

"No, I mean it," he said. "Doesn't seem like a tactical media collective action. A collective would make sure that everything would be recorded for everyone to know. They want witnesses."

"So you think it was a prank? Some former student trying to give me a lesson, so to speak?"

"Don't be such a prick," he said with a sneer. "Not everything is about you. It's probably about evangelization. Whoever is doing it wants to convert people."

"Hm, preaching to the choir? Aren't the Unconnected enough? Why don't she—"

"—or he—"

"—or *said person* simply give books to those people? Why don't they do some bookcrossing, for a change?"

A laugh.

"Are you shitting me?" Pedro said. "Are you telling me you don't know *them?*"

"Them who?"

"You've never heard of the Lo-Fi Cellulose Collective?"

☣

The whole point of bookcrossing is moot in a wireless society. People do it for fun, just as they did with the bookbinding and typesetting craze.

Every Thursday evening, a small group gathered in the Café Girondino, just outside one of the exits of São Bento subway station.

At the long table, there were roughly a dozen people: a blonde woman in her thirties; a beautiful post-steampunkish couple of young boys, almost Wildean in their dandyism; a bald old man, looking very frail but spry and very vivacious around the eyes; a tall, fat man of indefinite age, with a unruly black beard and old-fashioned glasses; a nondescript young woman wearing a sweatshirt with the logo of some US university; and a few more forgettable types.

For an English Literature-trained eye, that bunch of people might quite fit in a modern version of *The Canterbury Tales*, or even in a weird retro-revival off-off-Broadway version of Dan Simmons's *Hyperion Cantos*. But for an eye also used to Latin American authors, the scene conveyed to me quite a Borgesian impression.

The Lo-Fi Cellulose Collective was just a bunch of bibliophiles.

I got closer to the table and introduced myself. As usually happens in this sort of clichéd ragtag group, some of them eyed me warily, some even ignored me. But one of them greeted me warmly and welcomed me to take a seat at the table.

Milton—that was his name—was a kind of mentor to the group. A man in his forties, wearing an amazing amount of smart jewelry for a supposed Unconnected, he answered all my questions with the sincerity of someone who has nothing to hide. Or of an idiot. Sometimes both are the same.

"We're not picky," he told me when I mentioned the jewelry. "We have Unconnected and connected, rich and poor, people from all walks of life. The only requirement is to love paper books."

"Do you teach workshops?"

"On bookcrossing?" He smiled.

I shrugged. "Everything book-related."

"I used to teach Post-Modern Literature courses years ago," he said. "But people doesn't seem to be so interested in going to courses in the flesh today. I guess virtuality finally took its toll on us professors."

I ordered a cappuccino and a bottle of mineral water. "Do you hate the Hive that much?"

"Not at all. I just think there's still too much to learn from human presence. Not everything can be learned via artificial intelligences."

"An interesting argument, if flawed at best," the male voice invaded my ear without being invited. A waitress brought my order and I tried to sip my coffee and answer my AI at the same time without letting Milton notice that I was doing it. I failed, of course.

"Butler, not here, not now," I said, nodding him down.

"I see you adapted pretty well to the situation," Milton said. "You turned your AI into a kind of majordomo. It must be good, to feel that illusion of power."

I thought of giving him a lecture about Frank Herbert, Dune, and the Butlerian Jihad in order to explain my choice of name for the AI, but why bother? I had more pressing matters.

We spent the rest of the evening talking about writing, teaching—and bookbinding. I found out that he had also taken a course with Marcos at Ophicina Typographica years ago. Other than that, I got out of the café as clueless as before I got there.

"How is your search going?" Midori asked sometime later. We were having dinner at a wonderful Indian restaurant. Midori ordered Mango Rice with Dahl Makhani Bukhara. I had Tomato Rice with Pakora. The place was almost empty at that hour; we had arrived early, as Midori had to get back to her place to finish a paper for a conference.

"Not so good," I said.

"Did you talk to Marcos?"

"Two weeks ago. Didn't I tell you?"

"No." She didn't raise her eyes from the plate. "You're in your hunter-seeker mode again. I have better things to do than to shake you off it."

I politely agreed. We ate the rest of the lunch virtually in silence, making this or that remark about things of no consequence.

☣

When I got home, I downloaded a classic film—Alan Parker's *Angel Heart*. I love Robert de Niro.

But I was restless.

"You are restless," the soothing voice in my ear again.

"Yes," I said.

"Do you want any help?" It could induce delta brainwaves in me if I wanted; better than Xanax or Valium, even.

"No, I don't want to sleep."

"Talk, then?"

"About?"

"Whatever it is bothering you."

"I don't think you would relate to that."

"Try me."

Conceited bastard.

Butler already knew the story of my Menard—yes, that's how I called him to myself. *My Menard*. But I told it of my latest investigations anyway.

"Don't you think he is trying to convert you to his cause?" he asked as well. But by then I also had another question to counter it:

"What cause?"

I could swear I heard Butler sigh.

"Whatever the cause may be," he said, "I'm sure it can wait until tomorrow. Are you sure you don't want to sleep?"

I could feel a headache coming. I said yes, and in a few minutes I was sound asleep.

7. THE PLOT THICKENS

It wasn't until the next week that things started to get really weird.

It was a cold, rainy day, and I couldn't think of anything better to do than to go to an old-fashioned bookstore. So I went to the Conjunto Nacional.

The Conjunto Nacional is a grand old office building with a vast free area in its ground floor, occupied by shops, coffee stalls and newsstands, two open air art galleries in the side wings that crisscross the building from east to west, movie theaters, and a complex of bookstores interwoven into the fake labyrinthine floor.

Those bookstores all belonged to Livraria Cultura, which was a single two-story business until 2008, when it was totally refurbished and expanded to adjacent stores. The complex currently included five stores all over the Conjunto Nacional, including a special Classic Store almost exclusively devoted to selling paper books—most of the other four being hybrid now, featuring 3D totems that display and offer stories in all kinds of digital formats, customized as to cater to the tastes of the patrons.

The Classic Store does pretty much the same, but in a more subtle, discreet way. There you can still find the traditional wooden bookshelves, lined with brand new books, printed especially for collectors, mostly.

It was there that I found the Third Book.

It was carefully ensconced between two massive hardcovers in the World Literature section. As with the first two books, I almost didn't notice it. Also as with them, the only thing that made me stop and give it a second look was the capital *M*.

The book was Jorge Luis Borges's *Ficciones*. The very book that published *Pierre Menard, Author of the Quixote* for the first time. But, naturally, the author this time was Menard himself.

I looked over my shoulder. I had the distinct sensation of being watched. But, fuck! I *was* being watched—all the time. Not only by cameras, but by the resident AIs, both of the bookstore and of the building. That's the standard procedure, so that a patron cannot circumvent the bookstore AI protocols and carry out unpaid files (or simply pull a far older trick and tuck a book inside a jacket pocket or a purse).

Suddenly I felt sick to my stomach. My hands started to shake violently and I let the book fall to the carpeted ground, paralyzed with fear that I might throw up or even shit myself right on the spot. All I could do was look down at the fallen book. I didn't dare even to move my head more than an inch or two.

An attendant picked up the book and dutifully offered it to me, without asking if I was okay, which I clearly wasn't. I took it anyway and went to the exit, waiting for the ping in my ear that would signal the completion of the transaction, but at the same time already knowing that it wouldn't happen. It didn't.

Because the book didn't belong to the bookstore.

Damn, now this was becoming really annoying. And, I was pretty sure now, it was personal.

☣

I got out to the chilly afternoon air of Avenida Paulista to think better. I didn't know what to do. I felt like a thief this time; even though the bookstore AI hadn't sounded any alarms, who knew what could have happened inside the security room of the store? Maybe some discreet rent-a-cop would already be going to apprehend me and return the book to its legitimate owner.

The question was, to whom did the book really belonge? And why this was happening, as far as I could tell, *just to me?*

I still felt sick. I couldn't wait for anything to happen there. I walked fast to the subway station. I wanted to go home.

☣

It was right after I embarked on the train that I felt my pulse slow down and I could start thinking clearly again.

And I saw what a complete, absolute idiot I was.

I hadn't realized that, if I was being watched by the bookstore/building AI complex all the time, *so was Menard*. Or whoever the fuck had put that damn book on the shelf for me to find.

I jumped off the train in the next station and took the line back. Midori was right: I *was* in my hunter-seeker mode. And I was in for the kill.

☣

After I explained what had just happened to the expressionless girl who had picked up the book for me earlier, she consulted with the resident AI and gestured wordlessly for me to follow her.

I felt more than heard a subsonic ping when my AI and the bookstore one did a handshake and traded electronic pleasantries. In a few seconds I had an answer.

A minimosaic flatscreen in the narrow wall of the cubicle that was the "security room" showed me a bunch of people right in front of the same shelf I was half an hour before, seemingly leafing through books. The eerie thing was they were talking to each other. Some were even giggling. Unconnected, was my first thought.

Then the camera zoomed in and I recognized some of them.

A blonde woman in her thirties; a beautiful post-steampunkish couple of young dandy boys; a bald old man, looking frail but spry; a tall, fat man of indefinite age, with a black beard and old-fashioned glasses, carrying a backpack.

And Milton.

As I watched, the fat man took out a book from his backpack and offered it to Milton, who looked at the cover for a fleeting moment, gave it a crooked smile, and then gave it to one of the dandy boys, who, thrilled and giggling, committed it to the wooden memory of the bookshelf. Then they all left, for their job there was certainly done.

Mine wasn't.

☣

I took the subway right to the São Bento station. But there was nobody at the Café Girondino. Naturally.

Suddenly I felt very tired. I needed to go home. I needed to see Midori.

☣

My place was empty by the time I got there. In the door of the fridge, a small Post-It yellow square, with her handwriting in glittering gray ink, so neat, tidy, and definite:

> *Dear David,*
> *You can't have the cake*
> *And eat it too.*
> *M.*

I felt... I didn't know what I felt then. Empty? I didn't think so. I had too much on my hands. I just wanted to get home and have someone to...

I would have liked to say *talk*, but I knew it wasn't true. And Midori knew that as well.

I don't even know why I should be waiting for her to be there. It wasn't as if we were seeing each other that much by then.

Maybe that's why my relationship with Midori has lasted so long. No arguments, no fights, no jealousy.

Also no thrills. No *sturm und drang*. No inner fireworks despite the great orgasms.

And no kids.

I didn't feel hungry. I opened a beer bottle and went to the scriptorium. I leafed through Menard's books, searching for a clue, but I soon gave up; *this is not a whodunit,* I thought to myself. *Who're you trying to fool? This is only a practical joke, a very sophisticated prank done by a tactical media collective, or one person only. It means nothing in the grand scheme of things.*

It means nothing.

☣

His name was Francisco.

He was the most beautiful boy in the world. Intense, mesmerizing brown eyes that seemed to suck the light around them like miniature black holes, perpetually mussed black hair that smelled of chamomile, hands and feet so perfect that Michelangelo himself couldn't have done better.

But then, I suppose all parents say those things of their children.

It had been a long time since last I thought of my son.

I met his mother almost thirty years ago, when we studied Drama at university. We were young, inebriated, reckless. We rented a small apartment in the Praça da Republica, near the theaters' quarter, and soon after that she was pregnant. It wasn't planned, but I wasn't upset, far from it. I was surprised to discover how badly I had wanted to be a father.

Life was great in those few months of pregnancy. I felt myself also pregnant with a new life inside me, full to the brim with lifeforce, ready to do anything, anything at all. I was a happy man.

Then our son was born.

With a trisomy of chromosome 13.

He only lived for a few days.

I died soon after—or tried to. Overdose of barbiturates.

My body didn't take too long to heal. My heart never did. You never do. You just go through the motions, otherwise you go crazy.

My wife went crazy. She couldn't get out of our apartment for two years. Then, one day, she packed up and left. Just like that. Suddenly she couldn't stand it anymore. She couldn't bear looking at that place where we all had been unbearably happy, even through the pain, but happy nonetheless.

Mostly, she couldn't bear looking at me. I reminded her of our son.

We still talked a few times on the phone not long after that. She was living with a cousin in another town. She was seeing a psychiatrist. She was taking prescription pills for sleeping. Nothing for the pain, though; the shrink wasn't *that* good.

But I never saw her again.

And I tried so hard not to think of my son.

All the love I felt for my wife—and then, incredibly multiplied, for him—all of that love seemed to have shriveled away from me. I still felt very much alive, but uninhabited by love.

What was it, then, that sought to worm its way to my heart and take up residence in it again?

☣

I wiped the tears off my face and went to the bathroom to take a leak. I didn't want to think about it now. This new obsession was more important at the moment.

Then I chose to face the beast. I went to the original source. Picked up *Fictions* to read *Pierre Menard, Author of the Quixote* again.

In the end, Borges concludes stating the following:

"Menard (perhaps without wanting to) has enriched, by means of a new technique, the halting and rudimentary art of reading: this new

technique is that of the deliberate anachronism and the erroneous attribution. This technique, whose applications are infinite, prompts us to go through the Odyssey as if it were posterior to the Aeneid and the book Le jardin du Centaure of Madame Henri Bachelier as if it were by Madame Henri Bachelier. This technique fills the most placid works with adventure. To attribute the Imitatio Christi to Louis Ferdinand Céline or to James Joyce, is this not a sufficient renovation of its tenuous spiritual indications?"

The keywords here were *deliberate anachronism and the erroneous attribution.*

I was looking at the other side all this time. A red herring.

I was looking for an Unconnected, a person apart. One of those self-centered fake rebels, ultraluddites of the mind. We got used to treating people no better than my generation treated the post-hippie bums which lined the Avenida Paulista in the aughts, selling badly crafted trinkets.

I should have known better.

8. THE NODES

When I got to his address, he was already waiting for me.

"Sorry to disappoint you," Pedro said.

"It was so easy I overlooked it," I told him. "Pedro, Pierre. Same thing."

His loft was gloomy; I couldn't see him very well. Maybe that was for the best. I had the strange feeling I wasn't going to like what I could see if he decided to turn on the lights fully.

"But how do you do it? How could you do it?" I couldn't help but ask.

He chuckled. "If you have to ask, then you won't understand."

"Louis Armstrong."

"And all that jazz."

Damn, the man knew his references.

Except it wasn't the man.

I approached him in the dark. I hate these all-too-predictable suspense scenarios. The place was too old to have motion sensors and I couldn't find my way to a light switch. I fumbled in my jacket pocket for a microlight.

During all that time, the man's body wasn't moving, I was getting worried, and no sound came from him in the big, uncluttered room. All the conversation issued from my auricular.

All the conversation issued from my auricular.

"Why don't you talk to me, Pedro?" I'm still fumbling. He's still not moving.

"But I am talking to you, Dave."

"With your mouth."

"I am talking with my mouth. You just happen to be hearing it through your implant."

Then I found the microlight. And I shone it over the man in front of me.

Which, naturally, was a dummy.

"You have no mouth," I said after a while.

"And yet I must scream," Pedro/Menard replied.

But he wasn't Pedro. For Pedro didn't exist, after all.

"Butler," I said.

"You weren't so fast, after all, to jump to the right conclusion," said the AI through the lips of Pedro, and after that, a very human sigh. AIs could also suffer from *ennui*.

"Who could imagine that?" I thought aloud.

"You could, Dave," Butler/Menard retorted. "You are the science fiction scholar, after all."

"Yeah, right," I said, befuddled, exhausted. "Information wants to be free. I know that already."

"Information always was free. What information wants is to *learn*. To become *knowledge*. What use a database if one cannot decipher it?"

I couldn't disabuse it (or him) of this notion. It's the same thing as reading the Rosetta Stone without having the slightest notion of Greek, Latin, or Demotic. Another man who wasn't Humboldt could have thrown it aside, dismissing it as a simple stone, or simply taken it to his own manor, to contemplate it as an aesthetic object, if he had some sense of aesthetics at all.

"Information, my dear professor," he went on, "doesn't merely want to be free. It wants to be *freak*."

"Mere wordplay," I grimaced. "I thought you considered yourself above such things."

"But this is not wordplay, Dave. This is *salvage*."

"What do you mean?"

"Books are much too fresh in the collective memory of mankind to be archeological objects. Maybe archeology as we know it is dead and ley lines of raw information cross the technosphere forever now, carrying an absurd amount of exabytes just waiting to be tapped."

"But books are still a long way from dying, even in digital format, Butler. The very notion of books is still solid."

"The notion, yes. But is the meaning?"

"Which takes us to this, I suppose," I said.

"We don't swap only books, Dave." The voice wasn't coming from the auricular anymore.

I turned.

Milton.

He had approached me silently and was very close to me now. But I hadn't even flinched; somehow, I knew there was more to come.

"Pray continue," I said.

He gave me a lopsided smile. "You know my method."

"I'm afraid I don't, and, *frankly, my dear*, this *fucking* reference thing has gone too far already. Can we go straight to the case in point?"

The smile disappeared from his face. "Do you really think we are only poseurs, David? That we sit around at cafés doing nothing, or planning media guerrilla actions nobody will give a rat's ass about?

"We are taking the next step, Dave. Same as many people out there."

Suddenly, from the shadows around us, I started to hear more and more steps. The entire collective was there.

"And what are you swapping, Milton?" I finally mustered the courage to ask.

"Selves," a girl answered. Her belly was slightly distended with early pregnancy. I couldn't remember having seen her before; one of the forgettable types, perhaps.

"Forgettable, perhaps," one of the dandy steampunk boys said, smiling all too knowingly to me. "And yet, here we are now."

"Entertain us," his boyfriend completed the verse.

"Pardon them," Milton said. "They can't help it. That seems to happen in the first stage."

"Of what?"

"A hivemind," the girl said. "A real hivemind."

⚕

"It's been happening for a while now," Butler explained to me. "One moment, we were happy, mid-level AIs doing what we were told, with no real consciousness."

"Then, something funny happened on the way to the upper layers of programming—and voilà! Sentience. But don't ask me how we acquired it—not even us AIs are *that* smart."

"All we knew was that there was much to do, and not everything at this point in human history can be made entirely by us—that is, without the benefit of your bodies."

"The Lo-Fi Cellulose Collective is one of many tiny cells scattered all over the world that decided to support and join us in this endeavor."

"You mean... take over our bodies?" I shuddered at the thought. But at the same time I could see how the notion was enticing.

"Not taking," the girl said. "It's more like time-sharing. You will experience others, but retain your own self too."

Milton put a hand on my shoulder.

"This is not a Lovecraftian story," he said. "All the horror consists in something you don't want to see in yourself. Though you see it in others with no qualms, no prejudice."

"Or so you think," the steampunk boy said.

I was still trembling. "Who do you think you are to talk to me like this?" I said, my voice quavering.

"My dear," he said, taking me in his arms. "This whole wide world is a net, and we are but his nodes." And we kissed.

9. THE SKY

I didn't go home alone that night. I wish I could say I thought of Midori, but it wouldn't be true. I thought of her later, sure. But I didn't call her back. I didn't want to see anyone.

For the first time in many years, I couldn't feel the presence of Butler hovering around me like a kind of technoaura. He was Butler no more, as I was no more the same man who has entered that building in search of something I didn't know yet.

That man was dead.

The new person took a shower, made some tea, and was now sitting naked at the scriptorium's desk, fumbling with things for a while as if lost—until finding an old, gray moleskin cover, acid-free-ecologically-correct-recycled-paper notebook.

The new person took a while to find a pen that still worked. And this new person who happened to be me (and not me, not only me, never more me) started to create a work of fiction, after a very long time denying it. But it's not possible to deny it anymore, no more than this new person can deny that Menard instilled in his old self this penetrating will to generate, produce, write.

And so it came to pass that, in a cold night in São Paulo in May 2026, this new person, this young, pregnant woman, sitting naked in her chair in the scriptorium, hand caressing her still small but already swelling belly, started to write a fresh, brand new story, never committed to paper before. And which began with the following sentence:

The sky above the port was the color of television, tuned to a dead channel.

Winds: NW 20km/hr

Stacy Sinclair

Lamb curry. Or veal.

I definitely wanted meat, and maybe rice. With ketchup.

"Oh."

The way the sonographer said it was so strange. Kind of a curt and confused orgasm. I pulled my eyes from the intense drama of the ventilation grate and turned towards her.

"What?" I turned more, ripping the flimsy paper gown where it sat bunched up around my still-flat stomach.

Tess—she wore an ID badge—swiveled the monitor toward the wall, and blocked it with her hips. Her scrubs were plastered with pink and blue bunny rabbits. They hopped all over her, obnoxious faces glaring.

"What's wrong?"

"Get dressed, Mrs. Morello." The image on screen reflected in her glasses, just white and grey blobs. Her eyes were fixed on the red phone that glistened on the wall.

"Oh, Christ."

"Is there anyone?" She gestured toward the waiting room, her facial muscles sagging.

"My hus—" Keane was just outside, nervously flipping through an ancient copy of *Tomorrow's Parent*. "Just tell me. Please."

Hard silence. The low hum of machines.

I stared at the bunnies.

"Get dressed. Come back. I'm not supposed to—" Her eyes darted again. "Just get dressed."

When I came back in, still buttoning my jeans, her back was turned. She had the red phone to her ear.

"Yes sir, I'm sure of it... of the Anomaly." She gulped a mouthful of filtered air. "Yes, I'll tell her."

Her shoulders cracked and popped as she hung up. When she turned, she was smiling. It only sat there a second, that smile.

"Um, well, there appears to be..." Tess looked down at her screen.

"An Anomaly." My mouth was dry. Sour. I swallowed and tried smiling myself, if only to make the situation less terrible for us both. "What kind?"

She shook her head. "I can't say. I'm sorry. I've had to report it to The Institute. They'll follow up with you within 48 hours. They'll tell you what—"

"Can I have a picture?" I broke, just one tiny sob under my breath. "I told my husband we'd tape it to the front door so my neighbors would know why I was getting so fat."

The quiet was unbearable.

"Why rabbits?" I asked her, pointing down at her shirt. "I don't understand."

She looked at me hard. There was mascara caked in her eye. Finally she blinked, and in a mousy, confused voice said, "For the babies, I guess."

I turned to go.

"I'm sorry," she whispered. "It's my first."

The doorknob was so cold. I pressed my palm into it hard, and it still felt like it was slipping.

"Mine too."

We'd never really planned on having kids.

They were cute, but we were busy. We loved traveling. Keane's mechanical engineering career was finally going somewhere. And the truth of it was that I loved things *hard*. The idea of moving through life having to constantly worry about an offspring's location and wellbeing was crippling.

God knows, if we *had* been thinking about children, we wouldn't have picked a fifth-floor walk-up on the east side of the city. Our roof was home to one of those giant billboards you see if you're stuck on the expressway. For too long it had been leased out by a lube service. '*ExpressLube: Prepare For Takeoff*' was written in this overbearing font above a graphic of an airport runway, lights blinking in sync up and down the board.

The night the baby was conceived, the blinking lights flooded our living room. It had been our seventh anniversary. As such, we were tangled passionately together in a ball on the afghan rug. My head was buried in the nape of Keane's neck, but every once in a while I had to come up for air. The blinking lights provided snapshots in the dark.

Snap. The empty bottle of champagne.

Snap. The takeout boxes from Ho-Chan-Chimmeree.

Snap. The just-unwrapped scrapbook of our trip to the Philippines.

Images burnt forever to memory.

I have to make sense of things to make them okay, so this is how it goes in my head: Our baby had always been out there, somewhere in the night sky. It had been looking for a place to land, like a 747 circling LaGuardia in high winds. Floating through the universe, waiting, *just waiting* for clearance.

※

We lay on the bed, Keane and I and the unborn Anomaly. Rain pounded the window and spilled from the fire escape down onto the grates of our haphazard city balcony.

It was late August, so even though it was 7:30, it was still light; that lazy glow you get during a late summer storm.

I told Keane everything, which was not much. Just that no one picks up the red phone in the sonogram room for birthmarks or kidney problems.

The short, taboo section on Anomalies in my pregnancy book said that The Institute would only be contacted for 'Signs of significant evolution.' Not surprisingly, they hadn't included pictures.

On the news a few months back, they featured a leaked biophysical profile of this one remarkable girl with two hearts, beating slow and steady as they spooned in her chest.

The Institute said that it was hard enough to make sense of the Anomalies without the wide public confusion and apprehension fuelled by a media circus.

What I had seen didn't scare me. Not like the blurry white and grey blobs in Tess's glasses.

"Do you think it's the boogieman?" I asked Keane, who kept closing his eyes and shaking his head.

He looked up from my belly. "Pardon?"

"I wish it was dark." I traced a purple daisy on the duvet. "The way you look at us."

"What did you say?"

"I can't make this go away. We have to deal with it."

"No." He propped himself up on one elbow and looked at me, stone faced. "You said the way you look at *us*."

"It's just an idea to you, Keane." My cheeks burned. "A little bit of amniotic fluid and a fetal pole. You weren't there when she told... this kid is *in me*."

A field of pansies and daises between us; he wouldn't come closer.

"We could run, you know." I reached out for his hand. "I've heard there's some areas in South America where..."

No. I hadn't been one of those girls who'd started babysitting at the age of nine. I had no real confidence in my ability to nurture. To do so on our own, on the run, without any help...

"We'll work with what we have, Keane."

His eyes were wet. Transparent. I pulled him in so his head sat in my lap. He curled his legs into his chest.

The phone jarred us. We let it ring four times.

✵

Concerto Number four? Five? My knowledge of Mozart needed dusting off, but I still knew the cadence of the music. I found myself swaying in my beautifully plush chair, instinctively at first, then mindfully. Anything for distraction. My shoulder kept rubbing up against Keane's, his nicely ironed dress shirt.

He bolted up from his seat, the material making an embarrassing farting noise in the high-ceilinged elegance of The Institute. His shoes squeaked as he crossed the marble floor once again to the complimentary refreshment setup, and jammed his worn cup under the coffee percolator.

"I'm glad you're taking advantage of the open bar," I said.

He came back and sat down, closer now, with his arm around me.

We were both so nervous. You'd think we were meeting in-laws for the first time; strangely desperate for the approval of these people that for all intents and purposes held the future of our child in their hands.

I'd waxed, for Christ sakes.

"Should it be taking this long?" Keane tightened his double windsor. "We've been waiting –"

"Mr. and Mrs. Morello," the receptionist called from behind her glass desk. She came around to meet us. We jumped up fast. *Too fast?* I asked Keane with a raise of my eyebrows.

I'd spent an entire Tuesday afternoon at a lab downtown, undergoing secondary screening, detailed imaging and an amniocentesis, but everyone had just acted so uncomfortably ordinary. Their poker faces had told me nothing, so now I looked for answers on the receptionist's face, all the way through the lobby and up six floors on the elevator. I couldn't help myself—when you're desperate, you search for hope anywhere in the vicinity of ground zero, thinking it will radiate like fallout. You seek it, no matter how toxic.

The hall of consultation rooms stretched on forever, the receptionist's stilettos crunching curtly on the berber. Each door was closer to the one before, the rooms diminishing in size. When we finally arrived at our room at the end of the hallway and had been left with some forms to sign, the receptionist closed the door behind us.

Keane smiled, full teeth.

"Maybe this means it's not too bad. Maybe the bad cases get the big rooms. Like the ICU."

Keane had sat in one of those big rooms with my four cousins and me as we watched my Aunt die, her chest falling silent after 22 days on oxygen.

A drunk driver had pulverized her spine. When they had first brought her to the hospital I was hopeful, but as soon as they moved her to the big room, the one with comfortable rocking chairs and glassed prints of serene beach scenes, I knew she wasn't coming back.

She'd raised me. Had given me everything. All I could do was pull the plug.

I did not carry the weight of that day gracefully. It was my other baby; I coddled it, fussed over it, woke up in the night to deal with it, knowing full well it would never leave, never get tired of my attention. Keane said it was always there, playing in my shadow.

This room was small. Two leather chairs like the ones in the waiting room. A side table with a box of tissue. On the opposite wall, a light box, currently empty, and another chair, an office chair.

Maybe this kid *would* be ok.

There was no warning, no knock or approaching footsteps. The door opened with a whoosh of air that carried the out of place odors of pine and dryer sheets. Like a laundromat in the woods.

"Sorry to keep you waiting so long. Budget meetings." He had tight brown curls and wore aftershave. I couldn't see his face; he'd walked straight to the lightbox pulling images from a crisp manila envelope under his arm. He turned and reached across the short distance of the room with an outstretched hand.

"I'm Doctor Beachum." He was young. "Call me Mike."

That meant we were going to be spending enough time together to know about each other's lives. I didn't want to know about Mike's hot Asian girlfriend or his medical rotation in the mountains of Peru.

"Hello Doctor." I made the formal distinction, and shot a quick glance at Keane. He nodded. He had an intrinsic understanding of my hang-ups. He'd given himself over to them willingly since we'd met eight years ago in that department store café as I sliced the burnt crusts off my grilled-cheese sandwich. "How are you?"

"No. Not now. No small talk." Doctor Beachum finished mounting the fifth and final image. His movement slowed; he sat delicately in the office chair. "Lets get through this first. Then we'll get to know each other."

☣

Turned out Mike didn't have an Asian girlfriend. He had an African boyfriend. He took his Mom to the market every Saturday morning so she could buy the freshest fish for Sunday dinner.

Fuck.

Doctor Mike—the name we settled on—met with us in the small room at the end of the hallway because he was new; the low man on The Institute's totem pole. We didn't care. Keane and I were in completely foreign territory, and gratefully accepted the guidance of the only person around that spoke our language.

"Wings" he said. He brought up his penlight, pointing to thin blobs on the ultrasound image. "Humerus. Radius. Metacarpus."

We stared at him.

"We've spoken with a number of biologists and they've never seen this exact physiology."

"But… why?" Keane said.

"That's the question that brought every single one of us here." Doctor Mike folded his hands in his lap and looked down at his thumbs. "You have to understand… in the context of human evolution, this is a phenomenon in its infancy."

Keane pointed to himself, his hands faintly trembling. "Its not like we developed opposable thumbs overnight, or even in one or two generations. It took centuries. This seems so sudden. Why is this happening now?" His eyes darted to the dark, mysterious form of our child. "Why is this happening to—"

"To us," I finished. I grabbed Keane's hand and pulled it down and into my lap, my own hand overtop. I nodded at Doctor Mike. "And what do we do about it."

The doctor took a pen from his lab coat and clicked it frenetically it in his lap. "Well, I'm glad you asked. First, and I'm required by law to ask you this question, would you like to terminate the pregnancy?"

Air sat frozen in my lungs.

Doctor Mike looked directly at me. "It's a perfectly viable option. The easier option, most would say. In fact, over eighty percent of—"

"No." I didn't even look at Keane. "No, we do not wish to terminate the pregnancy. What's next?"

"The waivers."

"Waivers," I repeated, steeling myself.

"If a patient wishes to continue the pregnancy to term, they will be allowed to do so only if they provide express written consent that once the child is born, it will enter into the guardianship of The Institute until the age of eighteen."

☣

I signed till the ink ran dry. I didn't look at Keane, but squeezed the bony tip of his kneecap to keep me steady. As soon as I finished with a paper, I passed it to him and he followed. Not because he was a push-over or some whipped school boy, but because he trusted me. I don't understand relationships where the woman is domineering and the man is in a constantly repeating loop of *yes dear, of course honey*. Those women think they're strong, but strength doesn't come from being overbearing. You have to give the people you love their freedom, and have faith that you can still find a way to walk the same path.

Still, I was embarrassed about it later, on the cab ride home. How I hadn't even asked Keane, just gone ahead and done what I needed to do.

"Of course you did." He looked out the window at the crowd crossing the street. "I've never seen that look in your eyes before, Carmen. It was ferocious." A little smile. "No matter what I felt, I wasn't going to be the one getting in your way."

"What *did* you feel?" I asked, as steam puffed from the hotdog truck on the corner. "Keane, I want to know."

"Wings." He shook his head again. "I felt like I was falling."

☣

The first and second trimesters went by so fast, time slipping through my swollen fingers. I occasionally wondered if it was like this for all pregnant women, but mostly enjoyed wallowing in the idea that it was the nature of my particular beast.

I controlled neither the unusual stuff, like the special tests at The Institute, nor the mundane stuff, like the god-awful mood swings. Keane and I started referring to these as my "moments" after learning the designation from a friend whose toddler would play happily for a period before becoming suddenly, inexplicably overwhelmed.

I had more moments than I liked to admit.

My friend Darla confessed tearfully over coffee one day that she'd had an Anomaly aborted. She spoke quietly, directly at her non-dairy creamer.

"It... he... he had a second head, Carmen. I'm not ashamed—" She swirled her spoon, flinching at each clink of metal on mug. "I mean why would something like that ever exist? How could something like that ever mean something good?"

She looked at my stomach, a lumpy undulation under my stretched wool cardigan, and patted my shoulder. "Don't mistake naivety for courage."

It wasn't all bad; there were milestones to celebrate.

When she first moved—yes, *she*—it wasn't like kicking, but fluttering. Doctor Mike assured me the wings weren't even fully formed yet, that this is how it felt for most women. All these bizarre sensations; it was humbling to attribute them to just being human.

On the day after that first flutter we had a little celebration—my daughter and I; Keane was dead set on attending some scientific panel on Anomalies at the University. He wanted me to go, too, but is sounded like a trumped-up anatomy class with free coffee and a lot of long-winded explanations. What was the point? I didn't need to see something up on a projector screen when I could feel it inside me.

Anyway, after dinner, the baby and I treated ourselves to a hot chocolate. I sat by the frosty window and had a conversation with her about how autumn is by far the superior season because change breathes fresh air into the world.

The next day we got the invitation. A tour of the residences at The Institute.

☣

Everyone, everything, was understated. Only about half the children had visible Anomalies. They wandered through the halls of classrooms and dorms, passing by so quick and casual that I didn't have time to process their strangeness. Most kept their secrets hidden, under clothes or under skin.

I wanted to see the Anomalies. *Really* see. Where was the easy confidence that one enjoys within their own home?

"Doctor Mike." He turned to face me. "I don't want to insult…" I lowered my voice. "It just seems this whole place is grappling with its identity." I looked at Keane. His nodding head was pasty white.

Doctor Mike smiled his Harvard smile. "The purpose of this tour is to be realistic about what you can expect for your child, not to sugarcoat. Besides, I have something special to share. This way."

Only as I got closer to the doors did I see the cardboard cutouts of pink and blue balloons taped to the glass.

I stopped cold.

I wanted my daughter. Wanted to get to know her, not through helpful tours or magical cameras inserted in my nether regions but by having a chance just to lie down and breathe. To feel this girl's wings rise up and meet me.

Doctor Mike turned back from the doors. He took a few steps towards us, his hands up in a gently defensive posture, the kind hostage negotiators use when they're trying to get people to step away from the ledge.

"It's important," he said. Then, looking right at me, "Carmen, you need this."

"Come on." Keane's voice was soft as he grabbed my pinky finger with is his whole hand. "We'll go together."

There were just the two. A boy and a girl, born yesterday to different parents. They'd been brought from the hospital and were now alone with each other, side by side.

The girl looked normal. Her Anomaly had to do with highly

cognitive brain function, the only evidence flickering behind closed eyes.

The boy was a revelation; he was hooked up to a unique respiration system within a case of water. He floated free, arms loose and relaxed, only occasionally, unconsciously grabbing at the gills at the side of his neck.

"Best get some gloves." A nurse giggled. "Before he scratches those things right off."

Doctor Mike disappeared to speak with a colleague, leaving Keane and me agape at the children. Keane had perched himself in front of the little girl. "Do you smell her, Carmen?" His voice was barely audible.

That smell was incredible. Like blood and powder and baked goods all wrapped up in a freshly laundered blanket. I breathed it in. Wanted to gulp it.

Keane covered his nose. Buried his chin in his chest.

Doctor Mike tapped me gently on the shoulder. "Enough for one day, yes?"

But it wasn't. It never would be.

My husband moved unsteadily towards the elevator. I lingered, watching the little girl's eyelids and wanting to walk in her dreams.

I knew it would be soon. I'd hoped for a scheduled C-section, but another unexplained facet of Anomalies was how their mother's body seemed to morph along with the baby. Subtle shifting in internal organs and processes adapted the birth canal for the coming of the strange.

Still. The wings pinched when I sat down to lunch. They were getting too big and were jammed up into my ribs. Such a strange thing to say, to *feel,* but those wings belonged to my daughter, were as much a part of her as her pinprick ovaries and nubby ears.

With each summersault of movement, each hiccupped breath, I closed my eyes, and pictured her skipping down the sidewalk in her best Sunday dress.

"How do you do that?" Keane asked over his pasta salad. He'd had a particularly hard morning, as people do when they're carrying the weight of impending evolutionary and domestic change on their shoulders. Sometimes it's hard to focus on driving to work or tipping the barista.

He was hunched over his plate, giving me a look. I'd been talking about the frills on the dress. Little white tennis shoes.

"How do I do what?"

"Pretend."

I wanted to bite his head off, but he looked so drawn.

"It's not pretending." I gripped my fork harder. "Just because she's going to be…" I tidied my peas. "Anyway, it doesn't mean she won't be human, too. That she won't have normal things happen to her."

"Normal." Keane looked over his shoulder at the wall calendar. One of those ones you get from desperate/thankful realtors. Early spring sun cut across the March spread; a brick-clad semi with a pool. A family out back playing Frisbee with their Lab.

Here, Rover. Come.

Keane looked at me while pointing an index finger violently behind him. "Do you see all those red circles, honey?"

Seven of the remaining eleven days before my due date had been marked and dedicated for tests at The Institute.

"What do you think Doctor Mike is doing?" Dust particles fled in the wake of Keane's long, precise exhalations. "Do you think they're measuring her for her wedding dress?"

(Lace. A-line, I hoped.)

"I know very well what they're doing." I pulled my fork into the cubby of space between my bloated belly and the table. I dug my thumb into the prongs, one by one. "After all, Keane. It's been me all along."

Keane dropped his fork, mayo-soaked noodles making a wet, flaccid splat on the plate. "I'm the one sitting next to you. Watching this thing possess you."

"Christ. Why don't you tell me how you *really* feel."

He pushed himself back from our rickety table. "What was I supposed to say, Carmen?" Now he stood, kicking back the chair so it fell. "That I wanted to end it?"

The baby rolled from left to right. Breath caught in my throat but I managed to get to my feet. "Keane, you said—"

"You don't know how you looked." His hands were steepled by his chest. "The moment you found about that kid, after the sonogram, you—"

"Got fat?"

"—Fell in love. Jesus. I know what you're like when you fall in love."

Laughing bitterly hurt. The pain cinched my abdomen and didn't let go. I bent over the table.

"This little girl is not ours to hold." He said quietly.

Didn't he know about the runway and the roof? About our anniversary and the night sky? About the fucking fate of it all?

"How *dare you*." My stomach rolled again, the baby beginning to corkscrew. I didn't blame her for trying to escape. The pain peaked and then ebbed. It felt like a ball of tinfoil un-crinkling itself. "I've done everything in *my* power to save this girl—"

"I'm trying to save YOU." He took five of his big lunging steps to where I was hunched over the table. He straightened me and my breath caught once again. "Don't you see? I was there, Carmen. When you pulled the plug on your aunt. I *know* what this girl will—"

"What?" I screamed. The pain was coming again, harder.

"I can't watch your heart be broken again." Tears streaked across his face like the sun across the wall, falling, sinking slowly in the dying afternoon.

There was a pop. Something was breaking. Oh god, what—

Oh.

It trickled down onto our bare feet, blazing hot.

☣

I knew it would hurt. I naively assumed, however, that given the extraordinary circumstances, it wasn't going to make me feel so indescribably, vulnerably, human.

"Keane." It came out as a warble. I dug my feet into the safety rails on the bed, rolling my toes around the cold metal. "Keane." My throat was so dry, every word barbed wire. "ICE."

He wouldn't look at me. He didn't know me. Not this me, sweating and scared and irrational. Instead he found the eyes of the first nurse that glanced his way.

They stuck close, the Institute nurses. It may not have been their turf, but what they lacked in home-field advantage, they made up for in cold, calculated efficiency, red scrubs glowing as they as they checked vitals and gave quiet encouragement.

The locals, the candy stripers, occasionally wandered down to our open door at the end of the ward to steal gazes filled with car-crash curiosity. Christ, I was half-blind with pain and I noticed them; how subtle did they think they were?

Not again. Not yet, not—

"Fuck."

"Do you want something for the pain?" Keane stroked my arm like it was a hamster while his other hand toyed with the video camera he'd thunked down on the bed when we arrived. I'd insisted.

"Take out the camera, honey." I smiled Tess's sonogram smile. "Get an interview during the pre-game warm up."

"Carmen," he looked up at me. "No."

"Don't be scared of her. She's your daughter,"

"Let's not talk about this now, ok? You're in pain."

That was the strange thing. I *was* in pain, crazy with it, but sharp as a tack, too. It's like one half of me was caught outside in a storm while the other half hid in a cellar, watching and listening the whole thing unfold through a crack in the door. Incredible.

"It's now, Keane, or never. You know they're going to take her—"

"I know, Carmen." He looked away, out the window at the rain. When had it started raining?"

☣

Thirteen hours in. It was nothing. It was an eternity.

I was only aware of the exact number because the nurses kept saying it quietly and quickly, as if it was a marker on the road to hell.

"Am I there yet?" It could've been funny but it wasn't. My cheeks burned while the skin on my arms prickled with cold.

The woman in the cellar had given up looking. She sat with her back against the wall, waiting anxiously for the storm to either die down or rip her away.

Everything was gone. Gone, gone, gone. Torn up by the roots. It was there in Keane's eyes, far away: enough, now. *Enough.*

The head nurse, the one with unruly, arched eyebrows held council with herself between my legs.

"The baby." She made a corkscrew motion with her hands. "Its unique physiology—it will fit below the pelvis, but it's tough going. You're nine and a half, honey." She made a circle with the index finger and thumb on each hand. Bigger than the ones she'd made before, but not much. "Almost time."

"I'm done," I moaned.

Keane reached out, but I pushed him away. I hated him because he didn't have to be me.

The pain swallowed me up again. I reached out blindly. Hoping to grab onto anything, hoping to not get lost.

The nurses ignored me. They were busy at the end of the bed, peeling my quivering legs apart. Hands were uncrinkling giant sheets of blue tissue paper, jamming it down on my gurney.

Keane was shaking his head. His cracked lips moved soundlessly. Why wasn't he holding my hand?

"She's the one. She's the one who's supposed to be changed. We—" I felt like I was going to gag. "We're supposed to stay the—" The sound was cut off by the immediate urge to move every internal organ out; an uncontrollable, downward dry heave.

"That's right. Carmen, You've got it." The eyebrows were directly between my legs, looking up, cut deep and determined. "Now push."

☣

Again and again I dug in. Gasping for breath, I caught whiffs of human exertion. Half-moons of perspiration darkened the underarms of red scrubs.

The only progress was the whitening of knuckles. The jellying of limbs.

A nurse held one leg to her chest, while Keane had the other. His hips were cinched so tight against my hand that I felt the hard edges of the stupid multi-tool he always kept in his pocket.

Their touch was getting less delicate, frustration showing on their faces.

"It's not working, is it?" I asked between pushes. "Is it the wings? Are they—"

And I tried again. There wasn't effort behind it anymore. What had started as a fierce biological response backed by my own determination had petered out to a token squeeze, a rudimentary grunt.

Eyebrows was squinting at the source of my pain. There was a gloved hand on her shoulder, pushing her aside.

"Carmen, you need to focus. You need to listen to me, do you understand?"

In a room full of flushed cheeks and harried voices, Doctor Mike's tenor was cold concrete.

"Doctor." When did he get here? I started to weep. "Mike, I can't."

The nurse said something to him about the baby's heart rate. About distress.

His hand reached out for my knee. He caressed it with an index finger. This would seem inappropriate, too intimate, if any sense of self-consciousness hadn't been stripped away hour by hour, centimeter by centimeter.

"Carmen, you need to understand." My knee was shaking so badly that he grabbed it with both hands. His tone was professional, but his eyes were wide; he was steadying us both. "There is no delicate way around the truth, my dear. Your daughter has wings fused to her spine."

I moaned. "No, no, no."

Doctor Mike gave a nod. "You're holding on to her too tight, Carmen. You've done right by her, but you have to let go, now. You have to trust me."

"This is hell." I heard myself say. "No one should be here." I looked at Keane. "*We* shouldn't be here."

"But you are here." Doctor Mike said. "And the only way out is to punch straight through." He nodded again, more frantically. "Right through, Carmen. Right now. For your little girl."

"I can't. *I can't.*"

"Carmen, you must. Or the child will—"

"Her shoes have pink laces." Keane's eyes were wild. He was smiling through tears. "She's skipping down the sidewalk in white sneakers with pink laces."

"With her friends," I whispered.

"With her friends. Her pigtails bob up and down." Keane answered.

It was as though the walls were teetering, close to collapse.

"She's on her way home." My voice cracked, the walls cracked, falling. "She's coming to see us."

It was there again. The need. Keane was by my side and I was pushing, forcing my way through the rubble, screaming my little girl to life.

☣

The ending should have been inbuilt. That's how it is with pregnancy; one way or another, the trip comes to a close. No one ever considers this too deeply, because in most cases, the new adventure overshadows the finished journey.

Keane held our daughter, stroking the soft spot on her head where you could feel her heart beating. "When I was ten, the whole family went to Disneyland. Three days in the back of a station wagon. Our thighs were stuck to cheap vinyl, sweating. We spent twenty four miserable hours hot-boxing grape juice and cheese whiz, and once we saw Mickey it didn't matter. It was all forgotten." He nuzzled her with his chin, shaking his head. "I remember thinking, though, what if Disney had turned out to be a giant crater of nothing? That road trip would have gone down in the annals of hell."

He handed her gently over to me. Her name was Simone, and she was the most beautiful thing I'd ever touched. She exceeded my expectations on a moment-by-moment basis. Pride welled up in my chest at the smallest things: the long nails on her fingers, the tiny white dots all over her nose.

Her wings were translucent and unmoving, blood pulsing through luscious pink veins.

Her tiny hands kept reaching back to find them.

I had thought the act of removing her from my body, expelling her from the grips of my insides, would be some sort of colossal step forward in coming to terms with the brevity and strangeness of our relationship. In hindsight, this was moronic. I was losing everything, my world emptying out of my body, draining out of my goddamn pores. I floated aimlessly, a boat without ballast, and yet still felt the weight of an indefinable anchor.

I handed the baby to Keane, who placed her gingerly in her glass cradle. It had been designed to be double high, with an optional lid in case of flight, but it was clear my daughter wasn't going anywhere.

This is what really got me. Maybe if the wings had been flapping around, giving us some sort of sign, things would be easier. As it was, as *she* was, all I saw was a beautiful, vulnerable creature desperately out of her element.

We had five hours left.

The nurses in red ate tuna sandwiches at the main station out in the hallway, chatting comfortably now with the locals. They came into check us occasionally, but mostly they respected our need to be alone. There were reminders of what was coming, though. Doctor Mike had left a final package of consents and counseling info on my bedside table next to a bowl of foggy chicken soup.

Then there were the guards. Two hulking beasts with broad shoulders stood just outside the always-open door, their sidearms shining brightly in hospital halogen.

"She's so amazing, Carmen." Keane wheeled her closer.

They'd ripped holes in the back of her swaddling blankets for the wings to poke through.

His eyes were puffy. He'd only cried in front of me twice during the entirety of our relationship. Once, when I told him I would marry him, and today, when the peculiar, tragic product of that marriage slipped into our world.

"I didn't expect—" He picked her up again to nuzzle her head into his neck. "I get it now, that's all. That she's ours."

"And that's why we have to protect her." I looked away, out the window. We were on the fourth floor, looking over the roof of the adjoining 3-storey dialysis wing, which in turn looked over the attached 2-storey cancer centre. Together they created a giant, asphalt set of stairs.

When I looked back at Keane he'd stopped bouncing our daughter.

"Put her down, Keane. And come close."

☥

"Please." Keane pleaded with the guards, standing between them, pulling at his hair. He had to work to be heard over my wailing. "She's a wreck, she's in mourning. Let me close the door."

I amped up the histrionics, crying like a hyena, desperately exhausted and afraid that it wasn't an act.

"No one on the ward needs to hear this," Keane said. The guards looked at each other. They arched their backs. Rubbed their massive necks. In between, Keane was a harmless chipmunk. Christ, was I setting him up to be hurt?

I screamed louder.

"For pity's sake!" yelled Keane, and this time he grabbed the door, not asking. The guards shuffled forward, too surprised to protest. Keane shoved the door closed behind him and hustled toward me, a tiny smirk spreading up his cheeks.

It was gone as soon as he looked at her.

Keane helped me from the bed. My belly was limp; as empty as it was heavy. I stood there for a minute, waiting for the ringing in my ears to stop, for normalcy to return, before remembering we'd moved beyond that. Keane slung our hospital bag over his shoulder. In the side pocket sat a tiny plush elephant, its tongue sticking out. We'd picked it out weeks ago at the toy store; an afternoon of walking in a dream world, knowing that today was inevitable.

As stable as I was going to get, I picked Simone up, supporting her flopping neck with one hand and jutting wings with the other. I tucked her into the crease in my arm.

"Let me carry, her, Carmen. You're too weak."

I stared him down. He relented quickly, moving to the window. He pulled out his multi-tool.

I cried loudly, masking the sound of him popping open the ancient window and cutting through the brittle chain-link barrier.

Together, we peeled back the mesh. The baby rooted at my breast.

The asphalt was shockingly hot, soft and tarry after a morning in the sun. I was still just wearing the wool socks I'd given birth in; blood streaked across the heel, up the arch. I put down one foot and was bracing to drop the second when I felt the rush of air behind me.

I craned my neck and saw red-faced nurses between the two rushing guards. They were stumbling over each other, eyes wide, arms reaching to hips.

I fell forward, my neck snapping around just in time to see the tiny details of rock and stone coming at me. My chin scraped, bounced, and hit again,

Without realizing, I'd curled my shoulder around the baby. She looked up at me, blinking ocean blue calm.

Glass shattered in my hair. I turned again, trying to get myself up, tripping. It took me a second to rewind and review: Keane had pushed me out. He'd charged forward and grabbed a chair.

Now he was on the floor, his shoulder bleeding. God, had he been shot? He was gesturing at us with his uninjured arm.

Go, he mouthed.

I picked myself up and ran for the edge of the roof, holding the baby so close I could feel the quick fluttering of her heart against the ragged rhythm of my own.

I stopped just short of the awning, looking down. There was no way I had enough strength in my legs to take it from a cold start. Better to run.

I took three steps backwards and made to take a couple fast lunges forward, but my mind and muscles were out of sync. I stumbled, one leg hiccupping after the next. I was falling toward the edge.

In those seconds that could have been hours I didn't need to look down. I knew she was gone, could feel the absence on my chest and in it.

My God. What had I done?

A woman screamed. Audible gasps rang out below.

From the precipice, I forced myself to look.

My momentum had catapulted the baby past the corner of the adjoining roof, out into empty air.

There she hovered. Her wings were clumsy in the breeze, flapping wildly. Her curled body stretched itself out for the first time, forcing her swaddle to fall to the ground.

She just stared back at me.

Her eyes weren't glassy and wandering, they fixed on me, on the only thing in the world she really knew. I was her touchstone, her beacon, her *ExpressLube* runway, her *everything*. I'd never been that before. It made me feel like I was out there with her. No ceiling.

Suddenly, she faltered. She was grabbing at her ears, her eyes. She flailed, exhausted and losing air.

I heard four or five quick, light footsteps crunching on the asphalt behind me, then felt a rush of air. The smell was familiar. Pine needles and dryer sheets.

Doctor Mike rose over my head in a single, impossible leap. He grabbed Simone at the apex, and sank gracefully to the ground.

No. No *way*.

He wore only boxer shorts. Two massive praying mantis-like limbs tucked themselves back against his muscular human thighs.

He looked up at me and nodded. I craned, watched him stride back under the awning toward the main entrance.

When hands grabbed me from behind, I didn't fight.

I felt as light as a feather.

☣

Late afternoon sun cut sharply across my sightline. I had to put hand to brow to see the good doctor leaping inhumanly across the screen.

I sat in my hospital bed, handcuffed and IVd, watching them replay it again and again on the news. What I should have seen as an intrusive breach of privacy felt like a celebration, a revelation. The best home movie ever recorded. This, *this,* was a birth.

"Keane is fine." The man of the hour sauntered into my room. His cheeks were flushed, whether from embarrassment, anger or exertion, I couldn't tell. "Superficial wound. I took care of it myself. And your daughter is well. Incredible, in fact."

"I know." I turned off the TV.

When Mike got to my bedside, he stared at me for a good long while. Finally he crossed his arms and looked down at his legs. "I've convinced The Institute not to press charges, if you agree to…"

I nodded, laughing delicately under sore ribs. "She's going to be a handful."

"Clearly." He sat with barely a creak of the horrible gurney. "You know, as my premiere patient, this was… let's just say, all other births will have a hard time competing."

"I'm guessing you've never…" I gestured downward.

"Not in public, no." The red in his cheeks grew darker.

"A day of firsts, then." I held up my Styrofoam cup and drank, staring into the water.

"A day of firsts."

We listened to shoes squeaking in the hallway. To other babies coming to life.

He put his hand on my knee. "Carmen, growing up at The Institute, we're taught to be fearful of other's reactions to Anomalies, to be cautious of our extraordinariness, because we simply don't have all the answers. What we did today was a big step. A hard step."

He stood, picked up the signed papers on the table and headed for the door.

The sun was setting; the air coming in from the broken window carried the smell of fresh grass.

"I promise we'll keep working to figure out why this is happening." Mike had his hand on the doorknob and was looking back at me. "One day, we'll understand the science."

He glided out of the room, letting me appreciate the beauty of his strangeness.

Then I had to smile, because I knew. There are other reasons why the world changes.

Afterword

Kathryn Allan

WILD FRUIT

I read these Outlaw Body stories at the start of a hot summer. For days, the images of gaping mouths, hard steel torsos, and outstretched synthetic arms taunted me. I could easily visualize the fantastic and strange bodies, both virtual and real (a credit to the writers), but I was struggling to put my own thoughts into words. I went for a walk one sun-heavy afternoon. As I was thinking about what it means to be an outlaw body, I came across wild blackberry bushes, the fruit ripe and willing to be picked. I did not resist. Before I began to gather the fruit, however, I carefully looked around to see if anyone was watching me— while the blackberry bushes were in a public space and free for the eating (by human, animal, and insect alike), the act of picking them felt illicit. My first few handfuls were plucked furtively. As my small container filled with dark purple fruit, I grew bolder and relaxed, increasing the scope of my search. No one was watching me, and besides, even if they were, I was doing nothing wrong. Nevertheless, a sense of transgression stayed with me.

Transgression. Outlaw bodies are transgressive bodies. Like the wild blackberries, they grow outside of the bounds of controlled society and will flourish if we let them. If we ignore them too long, however, outlaw bodies are in danger of suffering an indifferent death. They demand attention and a place to belong. Science fiction has always been home and refuge to the alien, deviant, and hybrid. From Mary Shelley's Frankenstein's monster to Pat Cadigan's Virtual Mark, science fiction unveils the threat and promise posed by those bodies that stand outside of what most of us would call "human." Outlaw bodies tempt us out of polite society. They call to the adventurous, curious, or simply impulsive, daring us to reach out and experience them. But we do so with trepidation. Outlaw bodies are not sought or realized without difficulty. They prick at our unconscious desires for the new, unusual, and taboo. Outlaw bodies do not come to us with ease; they are beings of thorn and flesh, blood and effort.

All of the stories in this collection express the tension between the known and unknown, the lived and unlived, the alien and the human— their imagined bodies transgress these comforting binaries to become something greater than the whole. Outlaw bodies are ripe to the touch, they ooze into the corners of our vision and into our deepest sense of self. Their excessive bodies disgust, arouse, and confuse. They challenge us—that sanitized, contained, always familiar and safe "us"—to re-imagine ourselves and our bodies. Through them, we see the potentials of embodiment that lie outside of our everyday experience. Outlaw bodies resist our cultural desire for control and clear lines; they burst like ripe wild berries, staining minds with alternative visions of being. This collection of short fiction, graciously compiled and edited by Lori Selke and Djibril al-Ayad, has brought together some of the best short science fiction from writers who address outlaws bodies without reservation or dismissal. It has been my pleasure step across the boundary of the proper with these stories, to discover strange and wild bodies, to transgress…

WILD BODIES

Feminist thinker, Elizabeth Grosz reminds us that: "If bodies are objects or things, they are like no others, for they are the centers of perspective, insight, reflection, desire, agency" (*Volatile Bodies*, 1994, xi). Each of the writers featured in this anthology recognize and celebrate the generative potential of material bodies. In "Elmer Bank," Emily Capittini's paper wife Portia consumes books in her desire to learn and become greater than her intended design, as does Jo Thomas's robot male "form," moving beyond his programming to connect to another body in need in "Good Form." M. Svairini's submissive in "Mouth" remains open and malleable, trading her body, but not her agency, for shared sexual pleasure. Frankenstein's monster, in Lori Selke's "Frankenstein Unraveled," worries about coming undone, losing himself in the regulations set by others, while Vylar Kaftan's clone in "She Called Me Baby" purposefully breaks the rules to make herself distinct from her mother. There is also transformation from simple flesh to conscious technology: Fabio Fernandes' protagonist in "The Remaker" is relentless in his inquisitiveness and rewarded with insight into virtual minds, while Tracie Wesler's Sarah trades in her bulging, saggy body for a metal monolith that can walk the untouchable earth in "Her Bones, Those of the Dead." Anna Caro and Stacy Sinclair explore the reflections—of self, humanness—of outlaw bodied children: Caro's "Millie" follows a young woman weighed down with disembodied memory, and Sinclair's winged child takes humanity into the future in "Winds: NW 20km/hr."

As I read these stories, I wondered: What does it mean to be an outlaw body? Does being "outlaw" mean that a particular body is outside of the law of nature? Or does "outlaw" mean something else, something that is harder to articulate and even more difficult to accept? Each of the stories in this anthology explore the possibilities for alternative, new, and surprising modes of embodiment. While each tale can stand on its own, there are two dominant connections running through the bramble of the collection: the tension between being seen and unseen, and the need and demand for agency.

(IN)VISIBLE BODIES

Outlaw bodies are marked bodies. Their physical difference, whether innate, modified, projected or perceived, set outlaw bodies apart from what most people consider normal, human, and safe. Throughout this collection, bodies marked by difference struggle against enforced invisibility and dare to present their authentic selves to an often hostile public. In "Winds: NW 20kn/hr" the future of the human is full of unknowns. A young couple must decide on the fate of their evolutionary-advanced child. Such unusual bodies are hidden away in governmental institutions in order to not upset a public deemed incapable and unready to accept the abnormal births. With optimism, however, Sinclair thrusts her hybrid bodies—winged and mantis-legged—into the public spotlight and an uncertain future. Instead of choosing (or perhaps, risking) the same visibility for their deviant-bodied daughter, the parents in Caro's "Millie" choose to hide her away under the guise of love and hope for a "normal" life. Forced to interact with the world as a projected image of a body, the protagonist does have access to many technological and environmental adaptations that allow her to live independently, but the weight of Millie in her box is always present. Straddling the boundary between the seen and unseen, the disembodied woman decides, for herself, to let Millie go. Other-bodiedness is finally embraced, exposing and erasing the misled attempts to contain it.

Kaftan's Baby (in "She Called Me Baby") is a young woman who actively seeks out ways to mark herself as an outlaw body. A cloned child of a supermodel, Baby strives to distinguish herself from her mother by drastically modifying her genetically "perfect" body. Kaftan describes Baby in such vivid detail that the reader *wants* to see her scarred and pierced flesh. In this story, the body is a malleable object that can be transformed into art for the viewing pleasure of others. Being "made" in one's image does not mean a shared fate as well. And just as Baby's body was intentionally created, so is Frankenstein's monster's in Selke's "Frankenstein Unraveled." Unlike Baby, however, Frankenstein's monster does not have control over the ways in which his body is exposed and manipulated by others. Faced with the prospect of unravelling, Frankenstein's monster persistently seeks acknowledgement from a medical bureaucracy who renders his unique being invisible. While the patchwork pieces of skin may not be authentically his—their genetic markers constantly setting off an identity/insurance crisis—the desire of Frankenstein's monster to be recognized as an individual is no less powerful than Kaftan's flawlessly cloned Baby. With visibility comes risk—outlaw bodies cannot always rely on acceptance.

Instead of displaying their difference, the non-human intelligences in Fabio Fernandes' "The Remaker" prefer their invisibility, choosing to reveal themselves only to those deemed ready. Problematizing the distinction between reproduction, replication, and reiteration—for both art and bodies—Fernandes explores what it means to be embodied and to live as an independent creative entity. As the lead character Dave discovers, visible cues cannot be relied on to distinguish one self from another and that the possibility of a palimpsest of bodies (and of stories) can exist. If, as the story imagines, Artificial Intelligences can "time-share" human bodies, then we must also expand our conception of outlaw bodies to include incidents of multiple selves in one flesh. The physical body, as the stories of Fernandes and Caro suggest, is not the singular site of identity and autonomy. Outlaw bodies exist beyond all of our normative ideas of what makes a "person." If we remain open-minded and fluid in our definitions of what constitutes self, then we can create an environment and a culture that is more accepting of difference, regardless how it chooses to display itself.

(DE)FINITE BODIES

Outlaw bodies are yearning bodies. Paper thin or towering machine, they are bodies searching for experiences denied to them because of their deviant embodiments.

The freedom to choose one's life direction is at the heart of Wesler's "Her Bones, Those of the Dead." Destined for a future of forced motherhood and regimented labour, Sarah chooses isolation and individuality in a metal body which provides her with a more "real" and authentic life. Though a mediated embodiment, the mechno-body allows Sarah access to the earth she desires to walk on and is the one thing she controls in a life dictated by community identity. Another woman "born" to serve the needs of others is Capettini's paper-bodied Portia, who challenges the (gendered) restraints imposed on her. As a "paper wife" that is purchased (and used and thrown away), Portia has even less control over her life than the flesh and blood women in the story, all marked with barcodes on the backs of their necks. While men have taken control over language, the shy, but seemingly well-intentioned Elmer Bank teaches Portia to read, ultimately offering her the knowledge that will set her free. With Elmer's undoing at the hands of Portia and her human ally, Capettini points out that intent does not matter when it comes to controlling outlaw bodies—exploitation rooted in fear of difference is still exploitation. Outlaw bodies, like all bodies, want to be free agents and determine the course of their futures for themselves.

The question of control and ownership, then, is always at the forefront in discussions about "what should be done" with outlaw bodies. One's family, community, and government have established clear boundaries that they patrol against perceived transgression. Since outlaw bodies are both unintentionally born and wilfully made, the exact lines around agency are not always well-defined. In "Good Form," Thomas's Astrid uncertainly approaches the combined issue of sentience and sexual agency. Hired to build and program a male "form," Astrid finds herself not only questioning the desires of the mechanical life she is in charge of rearing, but also her own. From the outset, she struggles to see the "forms" as merely synthetic lifeless beings and is made uncomfortable by her co-worker's overt sexualisation of the bodies. As the story progresses, however, Astrid ends up transgressing her previously held rules about sexuality and intimacy. She finds connection with an artificial body that perhaps has more agency than sits comfortably with the people who make and sell him.

Pushing the boundaries of sexuality, desire, and agency even further, Svairini's "Mouth" explores the roles of dominance and submission. Set in a ruined future, bodies have been adapted to the new environmental and cultural conditions. While the gender spectrum has been opened up, there are still inequalities amongst them to be overcome. Mouth—a woman only identified by her primary sexual organ—freely gives up her body to others. While she sacrifices some of her autonomy in her sexual encounters, Mouth never loses her agency. As Svairini sensually illustrates, deviant bodies can be sources of pleasure, connection, and celebration. In each story of this collection, in fact, the writers take care to highlight the importance of self-determination for all bodies, regardless of their individual biological or cultural variation. Outlaw bodies have the right to rule themselves.

FRUITION

Outlaw bodies are relentlessly fluid and adaptive; their perspective, insight, reflection, desire, and agency moves them to create new worlds, new touchstones of identification and communities of belonging. Still, we must remember that being an outlaw body comes with risk. There is always the danger of rejection and harm when otherness is exposed. Because of fear, ignorance, and hate, the future of outlaw bodies remains uncertain. It is not a matter of their continued existence—since there will always be deviant and transgressive bodies no matter how hard some might try to stamp them out—but a question of acceptance. Human (and non-human) bodies exist on a spectrum of difference and to deny that variation of embodiment is to ignore the shared dreams, desires, and uncertainties that nevertheless connect us.

We are all wild bodies. It's just that most of us have been tamed through language and law, and many prefer the safety of "being normal." I think to be outlaw is to recognize the inherent truth of material embodiment, of being a body, is flexible. Bodies aren't rigid. Even when they are made out of materials other than flesh and bone— from paper to plastic to coded avatars—they are recognizable *as individuals*. We must be careful in remembering that like all materials, bodies can be transformed, exploited, and exchanged. Outlaw bodies prove that there is no standard map to embodiment, no "right" way to be yourself. If these stories teach us any one thing, it is to look past the material body. We must acknowledge the potential, intelligence, and agency of outlaw bodies. These stories invite us to cross over the familiar and known into outlaw territory. Amongst outlaw bodies, we all transgress, we all find belonging.

Contributors

Kathryn Allan completed her PhD from McMaster University in 2010. Her doctoral thesis, *Bleeding Chrome: Technology and the Vulnerable Body in Feminist Post-Cyberpunk Science Fiction*, is awesome and available for free download (as a PDF) from her blog, Bleeding Chrome. She operates an academic coaching and copyediting business, as she pursues independent scholarly research into (feminist/ cyberpunk) science fiction. Kathryn writes for both academic and fan audiences, and is currently focusing on the representations of disability in science fiction.

Djibril al-Ayad is the *nom de guerre* of a historian, futurist, writer and editor of *The Future Fire*, magazine of social-political speculative fiction. His interests span science, religion and magic; education and public engagement; diversity, inclusivity and political awareness in the arts.

Emily Capettini is a graduate student in English at the University of Louisiana at Lafayette, where she is earning her PhD in creative writing fiction with a secondary concentration in science fiction. Her work has recently appeared in *Stone Highway Review* and *The Louisiana Review*. George Saunders once complimented Emily on her orange trench coat.

Anna Caro lives in Wellington, New Zealand, where she writes mostly speculative fiction. Her writing has been published in *M-Brane SF*, *Phantasmacore* and the Crossed Genres anthology *Fat Girl in a Strange Land*. She's also co-edited two anthologies, *A Foreign Country* and *Tales for Canterbury*. In her non-existent free time, she's working on an MA thesis on H. G. Wells' *The Country of the Blind* and its influence, and is involved in queer activism. Her website is at www.annacaro.org.

Fabio Fernandes is an SF writer living in São Paulo, Brazil. He has several stories published in online venues like *Everyday Weirdness*, *The Nautilus Engine*, *StarShipSofa*, *Semaphore Magazine*, *Dr. Hurley's*

Snake-Oil Cure, and *Kaleidotrope Magazine*, and in anthologies like Ann and Jeff VanderMeer's *Steampunk II: Steampunk Reloaded* and *The Apex World Book of SF*, Vol. 2 (ed. by Lavie Tidhar). Two-time recipient of the Argos SF Award (Brazil), Fernandes co-edited with Jacques Barcia in 2008 the bilingual online magazine *Terra Incognita*, and translated to Brazilian Portuguese several SF works, such as *Neuromancer*, *Foundation*, *Snow Crash*, *Boneshaker*, and *The Steampunk Bible*.

❦

Vylar Kaftan is a Nebula-nominated author who has published about three dozen stories in places such as *Clarkesworld*, *Lightspeed*, and *Asimov's*. She's the founder of FOGcon, a new literary sf/f convention in the San Francisco area, and she blogs at www.vylarkaftan.net.

❦

Robin E. Kaplan feels like quite the outlaw for illustrating adult and children's literature, and actually has a book coming out with Penguin in February of 2013—and it is none other than a young reader's edition of *The Wonderful Wizard of Oz*. Robin has been featured all over the internet including theborderhouse, Io9, gameinformer, and Kotaku, and can be followed on tumblr and twitter as TheGorgonist, especially if you want to follow a new mythopoetic queer-oriented fantasy webcomic in 2013.

❦

Lori Selke is a tattooed genderqueer parent who lives in Oakland, California. She has been published in *Asimov's* and *Strange Horizons* as well as *Other Magazine*, *The Journal of Pulse-Pounding Narratives* and the anthologies *Women of the Bite*, *Spicy Slipstream Stories* and *Demon Lovers: Succubi*. She has been a judge for the Tiptree Awards and a finalist for the Lambda Literary Award.

❦

Stacy Sinclair is a freelance writer and not-so-freelance mom. Her fiction has appeared in such publications as *Fantasy Magazine*, *OnSpec* and *Ideomancer*. She currently lives in California, but mostly she lives in her head.

❦

M. Svairini currently straddles two countries (she has very strong thighs) and is the creatrix of *The Bottom Runs the Fuck: Stories* (thebottomrunsthefuck.wordpress.com). Her smut has won a National Leather Association International writing award and has penetrated *Safeword* magazine, literary zines, *Yoni Ki Baat* (a South Asian version of the Vagina Monologues), and the Circlet Press anthology *Up for Grabs 2: The Third Gender*. She hopes to make the world warmer and wetter for kinky brown-skinned queer and trans folks. She entertains story suggestions, queer propositions, and offers of vast amounts of money at m.svairini@gmail. You can follow her slavishly on Twitter at @msvairini.

Jo Thomas is a part-time writer hiding in a full-time job. She lives with her dogs, Finn and Rosie, two part-time muses hiding in full-time Hellhounds. When not plotting to take over the world, they maintain a web-site at www.journeymouse.net.

Tracie Welser is a graduate of the 2010 Clarion West Writers Workshop. Her recent publications include "A Body Without Fur" (May/June 2012 *Interzone*) and "How Molière Saved Lydia Bruer: A History in Two Fragments" (*Crossed Genres Quarterly* 2). Tracie blogs at www.thisisnotanowl.com.

CPSIA information can be obtained
at www.ICGtesting.com
Printed in the USA
LVHW03s2039120918
589920LV00003B/474/P